KILLING some TIme

Book Two of the Time Keeper's Saga

Cory and Zachary Barber

WORMHOLE BROS.

Cory would like to dedicate this book to Zach, because it wouldn't exist without him.

Zach would like to dedicate this book to Abraham Lincoln, without whom it also wouldn't exist.

contents

NOTE FROM THE AUTHORS

Killing Some Time—the second book in our *Time Keeper's Saga*—took my brother and me just over a year and a half to complete. We approached it the same way we wrote *This Was a Bad Idea:* blindly passing the story back and forth, with zero communication and no agreed-upon ending.

Originally, this book wasn't meant to be a sequel at all. It was intended to be a more serious, standalone story—grounded more in reality than science fiction. Truly flying by the seats of our pants, we managed to write about half of the story in just a few months. But when both of us hit a wall, I was the first to derail the reality train and hop back onto the sci-fi craft. We started an alternate version of the second half, but then we promptly shelved it when we realized it had drifted too far off course.

That's when I had the idea to merge the story with the world we'd already built in *This Was a Bad Idea*. It was a major twist—but ultimately a fitting one (I hope...)

An earlier version of this book was titled *Even Shadows Have Shadows*, which we still agree is a pretty great name, but it didn't survive into this iteration. Zach also created the original cover (the background of this page) in Microsoft Paint. A true artifact. We will always remember that gem.

While *Killing Some Time* leans slightly darker and more serious than the first book, the stories are deeply connected, and we hope it all comes together in a way that makes sense—and feels worth the journey.

We hope you enjoy this sliver of our minds, made manifest.

Much love,

-The Bros.

Note: ___C___ or ___Z____ denotes an author change.

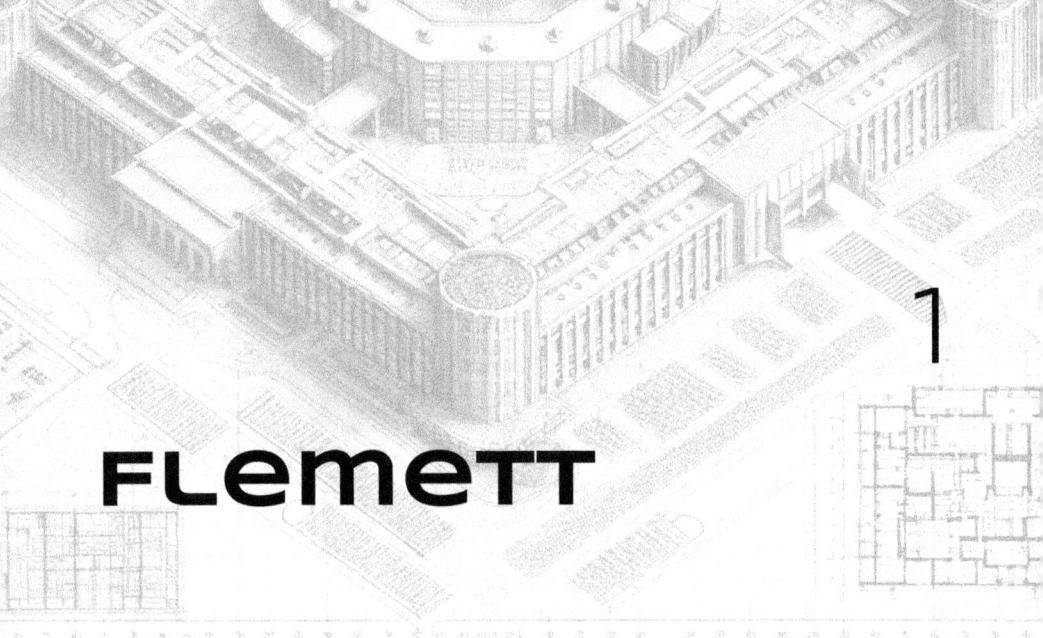

FLemeTT

___Z___ AFTER AN INTENSE workout, Taylor Frye gathered his belongings and made his way to the showers.

The Warden, Albert Oliver, stopped him in the hallway. The Warden was a tall man, almost seven feet. He was rambling about something or other, as usual.

Taylor wasn't processing a word of what he was saying. His mind raced as he felt the ground tremble beneath his feet.

"Sorry, sir. I must go."

He eyed the nearby clock on the wall.

7:30 pm: the most dangerous time at Flemett Maximum Security Prison. He needed to get back to his cell.

'No shower tonight,' he thought.

He scampered back to his cell, humming a song he'd come up with on the fly about smelly armpits. The song helped to quell the fear that loomed as he dashed through the hall, but it *was* quite catchy.

Three minutes passed as the New York coal trains chugged by the prison. "The Innocent Three," some called it. Within this short time, inmates used their handcrafted shivs. They robbed cells, settled every grudge, and evened every score. The walls rattled, and the train drowned out all sounds. Its deep rumble masked any crimes taking place.

Taylor sat on his cell bed. His hand clutched a broken piece of a crayon box under his bedsheet. The makeshift shiv might not even work, he'd thought, but at least it served as mental protection.

His eyes danced back and forth, analyzing the surroundings and looking for any threats. He noticed bothersome sounds coming from the adjacent cell and peered over at it.

A Bangladeshi man named Ferri Kamara was on his knees in his cell. Another inmate stood over him. Ferri's head snapped from side to side as the shadowy figure struck him again and again. Taylor and Ferri had spoken before, but their relationship rested on almost nothing.

It was clear from Ferri's humiliated expression that the abuse had been going on for a long time, and he had accepted the beatings as routine. Ferri didn't even struggle as every hit cracked against his skull. This terror was part of his life. Taylor could see it on Ferri's face. He wore the same expression he had at any other time of day—a lifeless look, worn by one just trying to survive in this hellish place that held him captive.

'Poor dude,' Taylor thought.

The guards were not present during The Innocent Three. The Warden described the moment as a cleansing opportunity "to wash away sin and promote a healthier atmosphere". After all, Flemett saw almost no crime at any other time of day. Only during this brief window did brutality rear its ugly head.

Taylor walked over to his desk and sat down. Pages and pages of incomplete books and notes splayed across its surface. "The Chronicles of Vanice Babesters" sat atop the pile. He pushed it aside, brushing the dust off a book he hadn't worked on in the last year—A Sign From Above. Did he feel like continuing the epic story of Otto?

"Hard 'no'," he said to himself.

Such a long day made focusing impossible.

An unfamiliar stack of papers caught his attention. They held together with paper-clips, and the top read *Intelligence Tests*.

'Strange!' he thought.

He was sure that he hadn't seen these papers before. A chill ran down his spine as he looked around to see if anyone was watching. He stashed them under a few other papers to read them later, when everyone had gone to sleep.

His thoughts went back to Ferri Kamara. Taylor hadn't seen the attacker's face, but he knew exactly who it was.

At first, Taylor hated prison life, but over time it drew him in as his curiosity took over. He spent his days analyzing everything that happened, decoding each visible and invisible signal. By now, he understood who called the shots.

He lived in what was called The B Unit, the "secure" section. Outsiders would consider it the safest place in the institution. To a visitor, it certainly looked that way. This area had more guards and more cameras than anywhere else in the prison. But anyone who looked closer would see that things were not what they seemed. The guards put on an act, exuding authority. Sometimes, they even pretended to care. In actuality, they were cowards who had lost control, and they had conceded power to the gang leader, Benny "Big Dawg" Andrews, and his mob.

During the day, Benny kept a low profile and behaved like a model prisoner, but after the evening meal, when the inmates could exercise or receive visits, he took over. At this time of day, his reign of terror was uncontested. As the prisoners roamed between cells, making threats and promises in whispered tones, Benny's gang kept to one side, its victims to the other, and some semblance of order persisted.

___C___ FERRI USED HIS pillowcase to wipe the small stream of blood that trickled down from his brow. Closing his eyes, he leaned back against the cold stone. He thought about his daughter, Maaryam. They took him away from her when she was eleven years old. Regardless of the "mountains of evidence" that they had against him, he knew in his heart that he was innocent. That thought weighed on his heart tonight like an anchor.

Today was Maaryam's fifteenth birthday. He had expected her to visit, as she always did on her birthday, but this time she didn't show. He reached under his mattress and pulled out her picture. It was a photo that she had taken for her eighth-grade graduation. It was the only picture that she had ever taken without her face covered. The contrast in the photo brought out the deep green in her eyes that he'd fallen in love with when she was born. Tears welled up in his eyes, but Ferri swatted them away.

Showing weakness in this place was an invitation to death. Only the strong-willed souls survived to see the light beyond the cold bars of Flemett. He glanced from his bed to the empty bunk across the cell. Gerald had occupied the cell with him since his incarceration, but he had recently been "removed from the count".

Ferri hoped Gerald was in a better place now. He shivered at the thought.

He often wondered what his life would be like when—if ever—he was released. Would he be the same? Undoubtedly, he would not.

His thoughts returned to Maaryam. He kissed her picture and returned it to safety beneath his mattress. He knew he would find no sleep.

He sighed, staring at the ceiling and prodding his bruised face with his fingers. "Keep your head in the game, Ferri."

AT 6 AM, DELIRIOUS and sleep-deprived, Ferri stood up from his bed and walked to the edge of the cell. The prison was colder today. Travis, the morning patrol, made his rounds, taking a count. Eli—a short, stocky redneck from Houston—accompanied him.

Most of the prisoners knew Eli as "the Farmer." Although he seemed uneducated and brash, he was brilliant. He had a doctorate in pharmacology but devoted his time to "slinging scripts" in the prison.

When Travis and Eli reached his cell, Ferri grabbed the cell bars and tried his best to look lively.

"Morning, Ferri," Travis said, feigning cheer and not looking up from his charts.

Ferri cracked half a smile.

Eli looked through his charts to find Ferri's current list of meds. He retrieved them, dropped them in a cup, and handed them to Ferri with a small cup of water.

"Bottom's up, Ferr Bear!"

Eli gave Ferri a once-over and squinted in the dim morning light to see his face.

"What happened to your face?" he asked.

Ferri played it off, swallowing the pills in one gulp. "Must have scratched myself in my sleep."

Eli stared, wearing a look of disbelief. "Well, by the looks of it, you haven't been sleepin' much. I'll put a note on your chart to update your script."

He scribbled some notes down and prepared to head to the next cell.

"See you tomorrow," Travis and Eli said simultaneously.

They shot an awkward glance at each other and moved on past Ferri's cell.

At 7:00 a.m., when Travis and Eli had finished the rounds, a buzzer went off, and the cell doors slid open. Inmates emerged like snails from their shells and moved towards the smell of breakfast. Ferri made his way to the food-serving line and grabbed a tray. Another inmate shoved him back, but he was too tired to fight today, so he took his place behind the man. He stared at the crude sign that marked the start of the food queue.

MENU OF THE DAY:

BOWL OF OATMEAL, SLICE OF
BREAD, ORANGE, CARTON OF
MILK, AND A SMILE

He muttered a few words of disgust under his breath. The menu hadn't changed since the day he'd arrived around four years ago. He shuffled through the line, eager to nourish his body, which felt like dead weight at the moment.

He sat at an empty table in the back.

"*Ferri!* What's happenin', my man?"

The voice came from Richard Muldoon, who sat with him every morning. Richy Rich had arrived in Flemett on the same day as Ferri.

"Keep your voice down, Rich. I have a *splitter* headache today."

Richard laughed in response. "Dude, welcome to my life! I can't get rid of my headaches. In fact, I might be suspicious if I woke up without one."

Ferri just shrugged.

"Yo, what's up with you, man? You look like hell," Rich said, noticing his rougher-than-usual appearance.

Ferri ran his hands through his hair and sighed, "It's nothing. I'm fine."

"Whatever, dude," Richard said, sounding snappy. "I don't care anyway."

The two ate in silence until the buzzer sounded for the morning brief.

They joined the ranks of inmates in line, keeping to themselves. Ferri glanced up as they entered the auditorium.

There was a new face at the podium.

Next to Albert Oliver—who always delivered the briefings—was a scruffy man in a suit. He had to be at least seven feet tall.

'Hello inmates, we've made a big mistake! You're all free to go!' Ferri thought, hoping for some good news for a change.

The inmates took their seats on the benches.

Albert grabbed the mic, and feedback screeched through the PA system. "We have a guest today. His name is Neel Holland. He is from the Institute of Criminal Research. I expect you will all give him your undivided attention."

Neel took the mic from Albert, faced the inmates, and cleared his throat.

___Z___ TAYLOR SAT UP in his chair, eager to hear what the guest speaker had to say.

Neel's voice jumped off the podium with such power that it was clear the microphone was just for show.

"Inmates of Flemett, last week I was sitting at my desk in Manhattan reading the newspaper, when my intern made me aware of 'strange...'" He made air quotes with his fingers. "...circumstances occurring within multiple prisons around the state of New York. Of course, given my position, I grew very curious about the circumstances. You may also wonder why I chose Flemett over Judon or limewater. The answer is simple: Flemett is the smallest, which makes a full investigation far less of a headache for my team. Questions?"

The room remained silent. Only the cooing of pigeons outside the windows was audible.

The Warden said, "Sir, please inform our inmates of the investigation's timeline."

Neel nodded in agreement. "The investigation of Flemett will begin in three days. My team will go undercover and be placed evenly throughout the cell blocks. I am not required to divulge any further information. Expect this to last indefinitely and be pleasantly surprised if it doesn't. Thank you for your cooperation, even though it is mandatory, and enjoy your day, Flemett."

Many groans emitted from the prisoners.

Albert grabbed the mic as the man walked off the stage. "A round of applause, everyone!"

A few inmates from D-Block sarcastically slapped their hands together, while everyone else began filing out of the room towards the yard.

Taylor glimpsed Ferri as they headed out of the auditorium. The man returned a glance. Taylor thought he saw a look of amusement in Ferri's eyes.

QUESTIONS

2

THERE WAS A REASON all convicted criminals wanted to be locked up at Flemett. Besides having near-perfect weather almost year-round, the yard was unmatched. A vacation for inmates; three basketball courts with chain nets, weights as far as the eye could see, and the signature Flemett boxing ring.

Although controlled by five guards and governed by strict rules, the boxing ring was available to all inmates who needed their quarrels settled. This ingenious implementation by the Warden helped keep Flemett at a countrywide low for inmate brawls. A mere ninety-two fights per year was a massive achievement, unmatched by even the strictest prisons.

That was all hogwash, though. The boxing ring wasn't the real reason for the good behavior. It was the clenched fists of Benny's gang that kept the prison in such tight order. But now, this "order" had grabbed the attention of Neel Holland, who knew that such a quaint prison had to have some dark, underlying secrets holding back the violence that regularly manifests in a prison setting.

Benny's gang had only two rules they abided by.
The first: absolutely no violent acts or threats until 7:30 pm.
And the second: stay off the basketball courts.

Benny believed that to keep the inmates under his control, they had to have an escape. A place where they could forget about his gang, forget about the grim hours that followed the train's passing every night. Grim was a generous description of the horrors that fell upon the inmates nightly.

Taylor had been lucky so far, spared from most of Flemett's cruelty, but he sensed this luxury wouldn't last much longer. He smoked a cigarette while he watched the daily B-versus-C-block pickup game.

Ferri was easily the best on the court. His dunk-pull-up game was sharp, and his hook shot looked like something straight out of Wilt Chamberlain's playbook. Taylor could tell this was the only place Ferri felt comfortable—the only place he felt safe. He spent the rest of the yard time watching the Bangladeshi man and wondering why he was here.

The clock on the wall of the main floor showed 7:20pm as Taylor walked up the rusted stairwell towards the showers. Luckily, his cell was close by.

During his shower, many thoughts ran through his head. One thought overwhelmed the rest. Sarah, his wife, had sent her first letter in almost four months, and Taylor was eager to hear from his partner.

Upon arriving back in his cell, he tore open the envelope. As he began reading, he noticed that the pages had crusted up with dried tears, and the words scratched in between the blue lines were almost unreadable. Only a few words required deciphering before he knew that tragedy had struck; a sad, familiar tragedy.

His wife had miscarried for the second time. Taylor crumpled the paper and threw it against the cell wall. Holding back a scream, he buried his head in his lap. Tears careened down his face, and life felt as if it was falling apart again.

The ground rumbled, causing the cell bars to clang.

7:30.

Behind him, his cell door opened, closed, and locked. Taylor's head straightened up, and he moved to turn around. If he were faster, he would have seen it coming. A large hand enveloped the back of his scalp and smashed Taylor's face into the wall. He collapsed as concussive darkness consumed his sight.

<u>20 minutes earlier</u>

___C___ FERRI LEANED AGAINST the wall outside the shower room, waiting for an open showerhead. He stared at the grout that separated the tiles beneath his feet.

A man approached from his left.

He shot a glance at the man's face. It was unfamiliar to him. His gaze returned to the floor. He wasn't much for small talk.

The man spoke up. "What you in fer?".

Ferri's eyes met the man's. "Excuse me?"

The man rolled his eyes and slowed his speech. "What. You. In. Fer?"

Ferri shrugged and turned away from the man. "What does it even matter?" he said. "Whether what they say I did is true, I'm still here. That won't change. Nobody believes me."

The man reached up to adjust his short black ponytail. "You thank yer innocent too? I knows I'm innocent. I ain't never had the know-how to do what them rat bastards are accusin' me fer."

Ferri stared hard at the man. Something seemed off. He noticed the man's eyes dart back and forth around the hall; he couldn't stop fidgeting with his hands; and he spoke clumsily. It was evident that the man was ill-educated and maybe even a bit mentally handicapped, so Ferri entertained the man's attempt at socializing.

"I guess that's what we all say, right?" Ferri said with a sigh. "I know we can't change our current circumstances, but we can make the best of them, right?"

The big man chuckled. He was a few bowls of oatmeal away from busting right out of his jumpsuit. "Yer right 'bout that. I'm Woody." He reached out for a handshake.

Ferri couldn't help laughing. "I can't say I've ever met anyone named Woody. Nice to meet you. My name is Ferri."

"Hey, I rode one of them boats called your name," Woody said, beaming.

Ferri laughed to himself. "So, what did you say you were in here for, Woody? I can't imagine a guy like you ending up here."

Woody's expression tightened. "They sayin' I messed up they computers or somethin'. I tried to tellum I ain't never touched a computer befer, but they put me in here anyhow."

Ferri felt an immediate connection to this simple man. "Hacking? Is that what they said you did?"

"*Yes!* Yes! They sayed I hacked the computers up. But I told them I ain't never touched a computer. They don't listen," Woody said, blubbering.

"Whose computers did they say you hacked?" Ferri asked.

Woody thought hard. "They said they name was F.B.E, or I., or some-thin."

Ferri touched the man's arm. "Well, it looks like we have something in common, Woody."

Woody looked up at him, and Ferri said, "We're both in here for the same reason."

Once Ferri finished his shower, he dried off and bid adieu to his unlikely acquaintance before returning to his cell. He hurried down the hall, trying his best to avoid any encounters that might get him into trouble. He took the most direct path to his cell.

Turning the final corner, a small but muscular man pushed him back. "Ferri Kamara, sorry to startle you. Actually, I'm not sorry for that, but I do feel a bit bad for slapping you around last night. Although you really should take better care of your possessions."

Ferri spat on the floor, hoping to seem confident. "What are you talking about, Benny?"

"I'm talking about the papers. The intelligence tests. The ones we came to collect last night. You said they were stolen. Well, we found them on Taylor Frye. Gave him a bit of a beating, too. So—like I said—you really should be more careful with your things."

Benny 'Big Dawg' Andrews turned from Ferri to walk away, but stopped to add, "Oh, Ferri, I surely don't need to remind you that the other half of our deal is due tomorrow. You'd best come through for me, boy. I won't be able to protect you anymore if you can't produce. Capisce?"

"Capisce," Ferri replied, sounding meek.

Benny strolled away, brushing up against the walls and singing a song in what Ferri presumed to be Italian.

Ferri peeled himself off the wall and finally made it back into his cell. He jumped onto his bed and lay down.

Staring at the ceiling, his mind raced. Benny was expecting Ferri to have another prisoner "removed from the count". He had given Ferri a small pill that would—upon ingesting— kill in mere moments. All Ferri had to do was slip the pill into Richy Rich's oatmeal tomorrow morning, and Benny would keep Ferri protected for the rest of his sentence. Protection from Benny could guarantee that Ferri would stay alive long enough to see his daughter again. But taking a life, even discreetly, was something that he didn't know he was capable of. He was sure that Benny had worse in store for him if he didn't do what he asked.

Ferri reached into the front pocket of his jumpsuit. A small brown pill rolled around the bottom. Ferri swallowed, imagining the deed, and hoping that the potassium cyanide would put Rich out quick. His eyes closed for the night.

Nightmares followed.

___Z___ EERIE NOISES ROUSED Taylor from a light sleep. He sat up, trying to pinpoint the source. The sounds were coming from Ferri's cell. Taylor was used to the nightmares that haunted Ferri nightly, so he gave the noises no further thought and turned over. He felt bad for Ferri, since he also woke from nightmares almost every night.

No more than thirty minutes later, Taylor awoke to excruciating pain in his stomach. It was by far the most intense pain he had ever experienced. He yelled out for help.

"What's wrong, prisoner?" One of the night guards asked.

"It hurts!" Taylor screamed in agony.

The guard ran over to the cell and unlocked the door. Taylor passed out from the pain.

TAYLOR LATER AWOKE IN the prison's emergency ward. The classic scene of blurred vision opening up at a hospital ceiling followed until a large-nosed individual gave Taylor's eyes something to focus on.

"My name is Dr. Joel Ellison. I am the Head Emergency Specialist here at Flemett. Last night, you were rushed in by two of my paramedics. They said you had complained to the guards about severe pain. However, during my examinations, I could find nothing unusual. This isn't just some feeble attempt at escaping your holding cell for a while, is it, Mr. Frye?"

Taylor shook his head in disagreement. "No, not at all, Doc. I had serious pain in my stomach. It felt like someone was stabbing me over and over again."

Both of them ignored the obvious bruising from last night's beating. That was a common tendency here. While Taylor neglected to bring it up because he thought it obvious enough to speak for itself, Dr. Ellison failed

14

to address it because he was afraid of the repercussions. At least, that's what Taylor assumed.

Dr. Ellison removed his glasses and placed his hand on Taylor's shoulder. "More than likely, this was just gastrointestinal flatulence."

Taylor tilted his head to the side, confused. "What the heck is that?" he asked.

Dr Ellison replied with a sigh. "Gas, Mr. Frye. A common occurrence around here after meatloaf night. All our tests came back with no issues. I can assure you that you are in tip-top condition. In fact, you are one of the healthiest prisoners I have examined in quite some time. Take pride in that, son."

Confused, Taylor asked how to prevent this from happening again.

The Doctor responded in much-appreciated non-medical jargon. "Take it a little slower when you are eating. Eating too quickly traps air in our stomachs. And go easy on the meatloaf! Just give your stomach a rest and be kind to it, and it will be kind to you. Lucky for you, you've slept the day away and missed last chow, so that will give your gut a rest until breakfast." He paused and gave Taylor a friendly pat on the back, then continued. "Alright, Taylor, I think we're all done here. There is a guard in the other room ready to escort you to your cell once you have changed back into your uniform."

Taylor thanked the doctor. He changed back into the fashionable prison garb, and the guard put a chain leash on his hands for escort back to B-unit.

Halfway to his cell, Taylor turned to the escorting guard, Officer Brucher, and asked to make a quick stop at the mail room. Hesitant but willing, the guard changed course and tugged at Taylor's chains.

Upon entering the bustling room of mail, a mist of musk and a bushel of words that would offend even the thickest-skinned slapped him in the face. Taylor approached the counter, at which sat a crumpled man who had nothing better to do than to fetch pieces of paper for disgruntled prisoners every day.

"Name?" he asked.

"Um, Taylor, Taylor Frye, mister."

"Do I look like a mister to you?" the man said, his words coming out of his mouth like a barking dog. "I swear if one more of you ungrateful slime bags thinks you can flatter me with this 'mister' and 'sir' talk, I'll take a crap on all the mail in this room and stick it in your dinner tonight. Now, how's that sound, *mister?*"

Taylor's mail fluttered to the floor along with his jaw. The disgruntled man tramped off to the back of the room to cool down.

The guard bent over to pick up the fallen mail and chuckled, "Now, why you gotta fluster ole man Gibbons like that?"

"I didn't do anything to that lunatic. He needs to be put in one of those old folks' homes...or a coffin!" Taylor said, feeling defensive.

Officer Brucher grinned from ear to ear. "Hahaha! He was always my favorite. Now, let's get you to your cell before the old coot finds you and gives you a paper cut."

"Open 2155."

The latch on the prison door unlocked, and Taylor walked inside. The floors were moldy in the less-trafficked areas, and the ceiling leaked occasionally after someone flushed the toilet above him. His bed smelled of rancid oysters. The springs were almost all broken. The only thing in good condition was the wooden chair, where Taylor spent most of his time. He would often work on his books, but had recently fallen in love with poetry, something his wife had always held dear to her heart.

He sat down and began sifting through his weekly mail.

- Letter from Aunt Terry.

-Memo from The Warden: ***All laundry must be completed by the end of the week due to scheduled maintenance on the facilities in the coming week.***

- Meal schedule for next week. ***No changes.***

- A letter to 2146.

Ferri's cell number. A piece of his mail had slipped into Taylor's pile. The sender was another cell number within the prison.

Taylor had a powerful urge to read the letter. Was it really a coincidence that Ferri's mail ended up in *his* pile? He held the letter up to the light, hoping to see through and make out a few words. But because of the thick envelope and the mass grave of bugs within his cell's light fixture, he couldn't see anything. He turned around to look into Ferri's cell.

It was empty.

Not normal, as Ferri only left his cell for mandatory events or the yard. The weather outside closed the yard down for the day, so Taylor was unsure where he might be.

'Doesn't matter,' Taylor thought.

He began prying the letter open.

Kamara, I'm sure you are having trouble accepting what I've asked you to do to earn my protection. Unfortunately, I have some bad news to share with you. I need another prisoner to be removed from the count after you deal with Richy Rich. This prisoner hasn't been here too long, but during his brief stay, he has interfered—-knowingly or unknowingly—-with our business on three separate occasions. Deal with Rich. Meet my associate, Freddy, on the laundry floor after second chow. Target's cell number is on the back of this page. Oh, and Ferri, keep your head up; there aren't too many prisoners who have it as good as you will.

Taylor flipped the paper over and squinted to make out the cell number in the top right corner. He balled up the paper and threw it across his cell. Scared and disoriented, he fell asleep early for the night.

2155.

A SCAR TO REMEMBER

3

___C___ FERRI WOKE TO a jab in the side—not enough to hurt; just enough to startle.

"Wake up, Ferri. You've got a new cellmate."

Ferri wiped the sleep from his eyes and sat up. The morning patrol crew was holding an odd-looking man by the arms. The man didn't have a single hair on his body. Whether it was a genetic condition or caused by an unfortunate turn of events, Ferri couldn't immediately tell. The scars that covered his body were from severe burns. Possible reconstructive surgeries had made him appear more human, but Ferri felt shock at how much the absence of eyebrows alone could distort a face.

The guards tossed the man onto the bunk next to Ferri. They removed his restraints and returned to the outside of the cell.

"Welcome home, partner," Eli remarked as the cell shut. Before leaving the immediate area, Eli stepped to the side and dragged his medicinal cart over to him. "Now let's get rollin' on the charts, gents. To the bars."

Ferri and the stranger in his cell stood up and made their way to the cell door. Eli gave Ferri a once-over, as he does every morning, and put his

19

tongue in his cheek. "That new script doin' ya any good, Ferri? Don't look like ya slept much."

Ferri snarled, "You don't say? *Why* do you even bother asking if you already know the answer? How the *hell* am I supposed to know if my meds are working? Isn't that *your* job, Eli?"

Eli stepped back and raised his eyebrows. He had never encountered Ferri in such a mood. He scribbled some notes down on his clipboard, gave the men their pill cocktails, and moved down the line.

Ferri sat back on his bed. The stranger in his cell had yet to make eye contact. Ferri considered this man. He thought back to the assembly room and the speech made by Neel Holland. Could this man be part of the investigation, planted here to spy on Ferri? If so, this could be a complication.

The stranger was the first to break the silence. "Let's just get things straight..."

Ferri sat forward and paid close attention.

The man continued, "I don't know you. I don't want to know you, and I don't like what I don't know. I don't like you. But I also don't want any trouble. So I'll mind my business, and you mind yours. Stay on your side, and I'll stay on mine. Got it?"

The man made prolonged eye contact for the first time.

Ferri nodded, but a question burned inside him. He needed to know.

"Are you part of Holland's crew?" he asked with minimal undertones of hostility.

The stranger began to quiver, and his face turned a darker shade of red. The scar tissue on his face appeared to inflame.

"Now you listen here, *boy*. I just said I don't want no trouble. But if you even *think* one more word about me having any connection to that suit-and-tie sociopath, I will *eat you alive!* Is that clear?"

Ferri drew back with sudden fear. A quick moment of reflection allowed him to observe his thoughts from an objective point of view. He needed to tread with caution around this new cellmate.

He nodded in reply.

The man, probably sensing Ferri's withdrawal, relaxed slightly. "Besides, even if I was one of his spies, do you think I would tell you?"

Silence drowned the cell once more.

At 7am, the cell doors opened for breakfast. Ferri wrestled with his nerves, which seemed to fight against him on every front. His hands shook. Sweat drenched his clothing. His breathing was rapid and shallow. But, it wasn't his new cellmate that caused his anxiety.

He reached his hand back into the front pocket of his jumpsuit. The cyanide pill was still there. Today was the day. Well, technically, yesterday was the day, but Ferri had chickened out and missed his opportunity. Last night, Benny had confronted him again to ensure he knew what would happen if he missed another opportunity.

He swallowed a lump in his throat and emerged from his cell. He sucked in some deep breaths and willed his body to relax. The less he thought about the act, the better. He convinced himself that nothing was different.

With a renewed resolve, he paced down the corridor to find the line for chow. After finding the line right where it always was, he took his place in it and scanned the mess hall for Richy Rich.

At least for the moment, Rich was nowhere in sight. Ferri continued to slide his tray down the line, accumulating a few splotches of food-like substances along the way. He paced toward the table at which he and Muldoon usually sat. For the moment, he ignored Rich's absence, even though it was quite uncharacteristic for Rich to skip meals. He whispered a silent prayer that this would not be the one day that Richy Rich missed first chow.

A hand slapped him on the shoulder.

Benny.

He gave Ferri a chilling look as he slithered past to sit at the gang's table. Words didn't have to be exchanged for Ferri to know that Benny would watch to make sure he got the deed done this time.

As if summoned by the energy in the room, Ferri suddenly spotted Richy Rich entering the chow line.

Fear paralyzed him.

His throat constricted.

His heart threatened to beat out of his chest.

He knew others had noticed his strange behavior. An inmate at the table to his right was staring at him.

"You alright, fella?" the concerned inmate asked.

Ferri pulled the collar of his t-shirt away from his throat. "Just a little heartburn," he said, lying.

Just then, Richy Rich arrived at the table and took a seat. "Ferri! My dude! You look like hell, man! What kinda nutty concoction does that Eli have you on?"

Ferri shot a nervous glance over to Benny, who was maintaining peripheral oversight of the interaction. A sly smile crossed Benny's face. Ferri averted his gaze with a quick snap of his head.

"*Yo!* Earth to Ferri, do you read?"

Ferri snapped his attention back to his target. Rich was staring hard, trying to read him.

"I'm fine," Ferri replied. "Just these new meds. I'm still adjusting."

The excuse seemed to work fine with Muldoon, who changed gears. "Sick, dude. That's what I thought. Now, let me tell you about this crazy dream I had last night," he said, full of energy.

Rich then explained his excruciatingly detailed dream that seemed to drone on forever.

Ferri didn't register a word the man said. He fondled the pill in his pocket. He formulated a plan, which was harder than he thought it would be, given the severe nerves and constant eye contact from Muldoon. He arrested a fleeting thought and put it to work. Interrupting a fiery scene from Richy Rich's dream, he wiped his forehead and squeezed in a remark.

"You know, Rich. I'm really not feeling too good. Can you refill my water for me?"

Rich sighed, either out of concern or disappointment in having the climax of his story interrupted.

"Sure thing, friend," he replied.

Friend.

The word stung. Ferri hadn't entertained the idea of Muldoon being his friend, but the moment forced him to think from his victim's perspective.

'Is this how friends treat each other?'

He shot a quick look at Benny, who wore a wide grin. The rest of the table seated around Benny "Big Dawg" Andrews were all staring. Rich left the table, taking Ferri's cup to refill from the water tower.

'It's now or never!' he thought.

Across the mess hall, someone at Benny's table threw a punch. Another punch landed in reply. Commotion stirred across the room, and all attention pointed to the gang's table.

'No doubt a planned distraction,' Ferri thought.

A few guards ran over and tried to break up the fight.

When Ferri was sure that no one was watching, he fumbled the death pill from his pocket and dropped it in Rich's oatmeal. He gave the gruel a quick stir to hide the pill. Letting out a heavy exhale, he sat back in his chair and peered around to ensure no one had spotted him. The fight ended, and everyone returned to their food.

Muldoon arrived back at the table with a full cup of water.

"Here ya go," he said, setting the cup down with a smile.

Ferri managed a weak smile in return and nodded to express his thanks. He trembled as he drank the water and listened to Rich resume telling his dream.

Ferri noticed Benny and his gang collecting their trays and leaving the mess hall. He wondered whether he should do the same.

Rich took a spoonful of oatmeal and chewed. He had no concern for table manners and continued to talk with a full mouth. Bite after bite, Ferri watched as his victim played breakfast roulette. He thought for a moment about what might happen if Rich *didn't* eat the pill or if he was found out. He pushed the thought aside and focused on acting interested in the dream.

In the next spoonful of oatmeal, Ferri could clearly see the pill peeking through the slimy oats. Muldoon hadn't noticed. He put the spoon in his mouth, removed it clean, and chewed. Ferri felt his breath turn to cement in his chest. He heard a crack inside Rich's mouth.

"Ow!" Rich said in a high-pitched voice. Then he laughed. "Yo, dude, since when do oats have bones? Jeez. That hurt my damn tooth."

He felt the side of his jaw with his hand, then slumped to the floor, lifeless.

___**Z**___ ACROSS THE MESS hall, Taylor sat unaccompanied and pretended to eat his breakfast. He had no appetite for food. What he had was a hunger for answers, and—like Benny—his eyes had been glued to Ferri all morning.

Taylor saw it all. The nervous twitches, the anxious glances around the room, the fight that attempted to create a distraction, the placing of the pill, and now, the limp body of Richy Rich collapsing onto the floor as Ferri exited the cafeteria with haste.

Guards rushed over to the body and called for a stretcher. Taylor couldn't believe his eyes. He never thought Ferri capable of such a savage act, but after seeing the body carried from the room, he remembered the mis-pitched letter and the instructions to kill. This was a problem, especially considering who Ferri's next target was supposed to be.

Taylor grabbed his tray, stood up, and went straight to the trash bin. As he walked, he heard other inmates mumbling to one another, talking about the warden poisoning the food and the investigation being a gimmick. They were clueless and scared, but Taylor felt calm and determined—calm somehow amidst the uncertainty at Flemett, and determined to save his own skin, at anyone's expense.

Since it was a Sunday, prisoners had no daily chores and had ample time to do what they pleased. Taylor made his way through the security checkpoint that separated the mess hall and the yard.

It was a picturesque New York day. The trees that were sprinkled around the yard had begun to shed their leaves. A cool breeze was now sweeping in from the north. Taylor moaned in disgust. He detested winter, and these were telltale signs that it was approaching faster than anyone wanted. It meant less yard time, which meant less sanity for all.

The bleachers that overlooked the basketball courts were barren, so Taylor made his way over to have a smoke. A small pickup game was in progress. A simple two-on-two today. Ferri and his usual partner, Corvin, pitted against the towering Atan brothers. The game was well-paced, but Taylor noticed something abnormal. Ferri wasn't playing like himself. Shot after shot bounced off the rim or missed the hoop altogether. The game ended with a blowout—a quick one, at that. The inmates had never seen such a sorry performance from Ferri and gathered around him in mockery.

Ferri stormed from the court and sprinted back into the prison.

Taylor threw his cigarette to the ground and stomped out the smoldering butt.

A brisk wind crawls up my spine

I sit and watch the newborn play

A dream I have time after time

To hear our child speak someday

TAYLOR WASN'T THAT GOOD at poetry, but he enjoyed it. It made him feel closer to his wife, closer to the life he wished to live again one day. This night had been more quiet than usual. Taylor hadn't seen a member of Benny's gang since the train's passing.

As he worked on his poem, he would glance up after completing every word to keep his eyes on the prisoner who had instructions to kill him. Strange enough, Ferri had been completely still for three hours, as if turned to stone by his new cellmate.

Taylor's paranoia began to subside with time, and he started to feel drowsy.

He put away his pen and paper, and folded up his poem titled "My Regret". A quick brush of the teeth and one last glance at Ferri's unmoving form gave Taylor enough comfort to close his eyes for the night. The chilly air in Flemett made it oddly comfortable to sleep, and Taylor was out within minutes.

"GET UP! GET UP! Everyone line up on the bars, *right now!*"

Taylor awoke quite furious, not because he heard the night guards clanging their batons against the cell bars, but because he had to leave an incredible dream to return to the misery of Flemett.

He slipped into his shoes and stepped out into the hall. To his left and right, prisoners lined up, half-asleep, all wondering the same thing.

'*What was going on?* '

Soon, Taylor's nose alerted him to the reason for all the commotion.

The guards moved with definite purpose, and just as one of them started to make an announcement, the smoke alarms triggered and a loud scream from the alarm speakers ensued. No spoken words were audible as the shrill rings bounced off the walls.

The guards slapped cuffs on the inmates and gestured for them to tail the guards toward the exit.

Taylor followed the mass of orange jumpsuits through the hall, down the stairs, and towards the main part of the prison where inmates got processed. Smoke filled the air as they piled into the small waiting area.

A quick brief from the Warden temporarily silenced the alarms.

"Inmates, listen up! There is an active fire in the basement that can't be contained, so we are executing an emergency evacuation of the East Wing. Everyone needs to listen clearly and follow orders carefully for the rest of the night as we work through this issue. Out-of-line behavior will *not* be tolerated, and deadly force—I repeat—*deadly force* will be used to ensure the safety and security of everyone involved in this emergency. Do I make myself clear?"

He paused for a moment to make sure all heads bobbed in affirmation.

"Follow the guards outside to the front of the prison. We have four buses waiting in the parking lot; one for each cell block, A through D. Follow your assigned guard to your bus and wait for further instruction."

With that instruction, the Warden put his face in his shirt and followed escorts out of the smoky building.

The alarms wailed again, and the clump of bodies packing up the room filed out onto the buses. Taylor followed the line of prisoners from B-Block to the designated B-bus. The chilly night air nipped at his arms, and the jumpsuit gave no protection from the bitter wind that howled outside of the prison.

Taylor stood at the end of the line, so he got placed at the front of the bus and had an unobstructed view of the guard. Eli was in charge of his sorry lot. He looked quite stressed.

"Everyone shut up and listen!" he said. "The Farmer" held their attention with his commanding tone. Taylor hadn't seen this side of Eli before.

"I am your guard for the night, at least until they get the fire out and it's safe for us to return. Don't even think about doing anything stupid. I'm on edge and will shoot your face clean off if I even *think* you are gonna do somethin' crazy. The Warden doesn't give permission to use deadly force that often, so my trigger finger is itching for you to give me a reason."

Taylor huffed. He guessed Eli needed to display confidence, being *alone* in guarding fifty inmates. The cuffs weren't *that* restraining when they cuffed you with arms in front.

"Now, with that said," Eli said, looking at a clipboard, "this bus is your temporary cell block until they figure out where to put y'all. I will do a roll call now. When you hear your number, say 'here' loud and proud, because I will not repeat myself. Got it? 2130...2131..."

Eli was only able to get through three numbers before a fight broke out in the back of the bus. He dropped his clipboard and darted to the brawl, pulling out his gun and popping off five shots into the ceiling of the bus. A mass commotion followed as the inmates jumped onto Eli and took him to the ground.

Little did anyone know, Taylor had already analyzed every aspect of this situation. As the numbers were being called out, he watched Eli, waiting. He knew the cooperation wouldn't last long when he was without backup. Taylor had also noticed that, in the heat of the stressful moment, Eli had forgotten to close the bus door. Taylor sat at the very front, with only handcuffs to hold him back. As soon as he realized this, he knew the moment he'd wished for had come. Seconds after Eli fired off the first shot, Taylor was already down the stairs of the bus, sprinting for the fence hidden by the trees across the parking lot.

It all happened so fast.

Moments later, Taylor was crouched down in some foliage at the edge of the woods, looking back at the line of parked buses. Inmates scattered like ants. Shots fired from multiple weapons as guards lost control. He glanced down toward his leg and noticed a bit of mangled flesh on his right thigh.

"Thought you could get over razor-wire without getting cut, did you, Taylor?" he said to himself in a whisper.

He pulled his tank-top off and wrapped his leg up to subdue the bleeding, quickly turning his attention back to the parking lot, which was still just in sight from his hidden vantage point.

Many guards had already surrounded the buses and were working on controlling all inmates onboard. Taylor was still close enough to make out words spoken by the louder of the guards.

"We're missing a few prisoners. Search the area. Get the dogs!" a guard yelled from the bus.

Taylor's heart felt like it might burst out of his chest. He didn't know what to do. Frozen in place, he watched the guards scramble—arming themselves, unleashing dogs, beginning the hunt. His mind buzzed, but no useful thoughts emerged. It was as if someone had jammed a rock into the gears of his brain; they strained to turn, whining uselessly as they ground against it.

His perception of time slowed down as he remained focused on his surroundings. At some point, a bark alerted him to an approaching dog. A jolt of adrenaline surged through his body, and he turned around to sprint from his pursuers.

Taylor ran for what seemed like forever, but the barking never faded and Flemett's lights never dimmed. He stopped and collapsed behind a large white pine tree to catch his breath. When he peeked around the trunk, he noticed a guard only three hundred feet behind him. Taylor watched as he let his hound free from its leash. It ran right for him.

He stood up and ran as fast as he could.

The dog closed the distance with each passing step until he heard it right behind him.

Taylor turned around and tried kicking dirt into the dog's eyes, but it was already airborne. The dog slammed into Taylor, and its teeth into the side of Taylor's face. They both collapsed to the dirt as he screamed out in agony, trying with cuffed hands to find a stick or a rock on the ground to hit the dog with. He could feel the canine's teeth tearing apart the flesh around his left eye. The dog jerked his head, and sharp pain lanced through Taylor's face. He flailed his legs and brought up his hands to claw at the dog's face, but it wouldn't release its grip.

In a last-ditch effort to save his own life, Taylor got an arm around the dog's neck and squeezed with all of his strength. It was an arduous task with the awkwardness of the cuffs. After a small eternity of thrashing, the hound's body rolled to the ground, limp.

Taylor grabbed his face and rolled onto his side. The pain was unbearable. He began losing consciousness. Just before his blurred vision faded completely, he saw a guard approaching, weapon pointed and shouting muffled noises. Then a thin figure appeared behind the guard and elbowed him in the neck. The tall figure tore the gun from the stunned guard's hands and struck him on the head with the butt. The last thing Taylor saw before he drifted away was the guard crumpling to the ground, unconscious.

___C___ FERRI STARED AT Taylor Frye's body, sprawled out on the ground in front of him. Slight convulsions of leftover adrenaline ripped through his unconscious body, causing him to jerk.

Ferri tried his best to calm down. Labored breaths escaped with whispered swears. He could hear his pulse throbbing like war drums in his ears. Closing his eyes, he exhaled a breath of physical and mental exhaustion. He collapsed to the ground, holding himself up with weak arms.

"Calm down, Ferri," he said aloud to himself.

He glanced down at his hands, which trembled like leaves in the wind. His right thumb had dislocated when slipping out of his cuffs, but he managed to pop it back into place after intense stabs of pain. His clothes dripped with blood from jumping the razor-wire fence. It was miraculous to have made it over that fence, but he needed to stop the bleeding soon.

Beside him on the ground lay the assault rifle he'd stolen from the guard who had tried to kill Taylor. He pulled it closer and checked the magazine through a slit in the side—six rounds left. Without looking further, he assumed there was one in the chamber. He wasn't versed enough to know how to check. He'd never held a gun in his life.

He scanned the area for any sign of a threat. Seeing none, he searched the rifle for a safety toggle, hoping to avoid an accidental shot that would give away their position. He knew enough from movies to assume all guns had a safety.

'Surely, someone had heard the shouts from that guard,' he thought. They would be onto him soon.

He crawled over to Taylor and poked him a few times to rouse him. He stirred and regained consciousness. Remnants of adrenaline surged through his muscles and sent him rolling around on the ground in confusion, fighting back against the handcuffs. Ferri held his shoulders and attempted to calm him down.

"Frye! Hey! Calm down. *We escaped!* We're out, but we have to get away from here *right now!* There's no guard on us for the moment, but if they heard the shouts from the guard before I knocked him out," he pointed at the limp body of the guard, "they'll be hot on our trail soon. Also, that guard will not sleep forever. Let's go!"

Ferri helped Taylor to his feet.

"I can't see a thing out here," Taylor said, sounding half asleep.

"That's because your left eye is crusted over with blood. Don't touch it. Just stay close," Ferri said. He could hear the fear in Taylor's heavy breaths.

They dashed toward the forest ahead of them. The guards would have a much harder time finding them in there.

Once they were out of sight within the tree line, they stopped to catch their breath.

"We need to stop this bleeding," Ferri said in a serious manner.

He slumped onto the ground and began the tedious task of ripping off strips of fabric from his jumpsuit. Doing the best he could in the waning light of the prison and tree-shrouded moonlight, he wrapped the left side

31

of Taylor's face, his right forearm, both hands, and a large gash in his right thigh. Frye's other injuries did not merit immediate attention and would have to wait.

Taylor did his best to return the favor, but the cuffs made the task much more difficult. Ferri helped as much as he could. Taylor's injuries were far worse than Ferri's. Ferri had suffered only cuts to his hands and forearms and a minor gash on his stomach and left thigh. With wounds bandaged—clearly by amateurs—they pushed forward into the woods.

They moved for several hours, relying on adrenaline and the will to survive to keep them moving. The night was at its deepest, and the cold further slowed their progress. The temp was still above freezing, but between exhaustion and lack of clothing, it was bitter cold.

Taylor collapsed on the ground. He was shivering and mumbling non-sense.

Ferri sank to his knees next to him. "We have to keep moving, Frye. We will die if we stop now."

Taylor shoved him away. "Then just let me die!"

Ferri looked around, hope waning. They had lost the ambient light of civilization, and now the only light came from the filtered moonlight above. For this at least, he was grateful. Continuing to look around, he noticed a very faint orange glow in the distance. The light didn't seem natural, but he had the notion that maybe he was being delusional.

"Do you see that light over there?" he asked Taylor.

Taylor's head shot up, and he looked around, desperate to confirm the sighting.

"Where? What light?" he said, sounding frantic.

Ferri reached out a hand in front of Taylor's uncovered eye. He pointed toward the faint light.

"I see it!" Taylor said. "I see it!"

Taylor's head whipped back toward Ferri's hand in a double-take.

"Hey! How'd you get out of your cuffs?"

He finally noticed, Ferri thought with a chuckle.

"Slippery wrists," Ferri replied, then helped Taylor to his feet. "Let's go. We'll die if we stay here. We might die over there, too, but we also might *not* die over there, so that sounds like a better option to me."

The light grew larger as they approached. Repeatedly, they tripped over fallen branches hidden in the forest's dark. Ferri's shoe kicked a small metal object on the forest floor. He stopped for a moment, setting down the assault rifle. He reached to grab the object. It glimmered in the dim light, intriguing him.

The object was cold. It didn't appear to be junk. He assumed it to be some sort of machine part. A small engraving on the bottom showed the word **Granradurhatinator** and a smaller, more crudely etched 'Gran Gran'. He decided it might be worth keeping to get a better look later and stuffed it in his pocket. They continued towards the light.

When they were finally close enough to determine the source of the light, Taylor said in a hoarse yell, "It's a cabin!"

Ferri squinted his eyes and slowly a shadow of a small shack formed in his field of view. A thin lamppost stood next to it—their guiding light.

Finding renewed energy, the two ran to the structure and searched for an entry. Upon finding a door, Ferri dropped the assault rifle again to grip the handle, and with his bandaged hands he wrenched on it.

"It's locked."

He slammed his body against the door to break in. The door held its solidity within its rigid frame. With each attempt at breaking through the door, Ferri's jumpsuit left a faint stain of fresh blood on the wooden door.

He heard Taylor speak up from the right side of the small porch.

"There's a window on this side."

Ferri moved in the direction that Taylor was pointing. The light was too dim to notice the abrupt ending of the porch. Unexpectedly, Ferri misjudged his step and fell face-first off the porch. Not catching himself with his hands, his face smacked the cold forest floor. He lost consciousness.

___Z___ Taylor rushed over to pull Ferri's limp body from the dirt.

As he bent over, a grisly voice behind him spoke. "Stan' up and turn aroun' slowly, boy."

Taylor turned around. The barrel of a twelve-gauge stared him in the face, and its owner—an elderly man wearing torn-up overalls—looked to be playing no games.

"Yer lucky I ain't blown yer head clean off already, scumbag. What are ya two doin out hea? Ya just escape the prison? And what in the Sam Hill is wrong with yer face?" the old man asked.

Taylor cleared the knot in his throat. "That prison is a bad place, man, but I assure you, we aren't bad people. We found the opportunity to give ourselves a new chance in life, and we took it. We mean no harm, I swear it. And a dog attacked me, but I'm fine."

A moment of silence passed before the faint sound of a police search party became audible a short distance away.

The old man looked at Ferri's unconscious body lying on the ground.

"Grab yer friend or boyfriend or whatever y'alls is and get in the cabin, now!"

It took all the energy that Taylor had left to muscle the dead weight of Ferri's narrow frame inside. Taylor propped Ferri into a chair sitting just in front of a small fire that crackled inside of a metal barrel. Junk cluttered the inside of the cabin, and old newspaper clippings plastered the walls.

Taylor could hear scrubbing noises coming from the outside of the door. The old man entered moments later carrying a blood-damp rag. The man slammed the door shut and locked the two deadbolts that held it shut.

"The cops are gonna come searchin' my place fer y'all. They always do whenev' some' like the sort happens. Ya have a few minutes to warm up, but whenev' I give ya the signal, the both of ya's need make yer way to the study. The door is behind that there grandfather clock. Ya got it?"

Confused about why this man was helping, Taylor just nodded his head and stared at Ferri as he regained consciousness. Just a few minutes passed before the man jumped up from his chair and peered out the front window.

"Go on now, fellas!" he said.

Taylor grabbed Ferri's arm and helped him to his feet. "Follow me and don't make a sound, alright? I'll explain everything later," he said in a whisper.

The two snuck towards the dust-covered clock and slid behind it into the small room hidden within the wall. It was dark and had a large armoire they could both easily fit inside. All they could do now was listen, and hope their new acquaintance wouldn't give them up.

A knock came at the door.

"Police. Open up. We have some questions."

The old man opened the door.

"What kinda questions?" he asked.

"We just had two inmates escape Flemett. We are just sweeping the area to search and making sure you are alright, sir," the cop replied.

"Well, I ain't seen any of them misfits. As a matter of fact, I *was* alright until ya just interrupted me sleepin'."

The officer cleared his throat. "Well, I'm sorry for waking you, sir. Just doing my job, that is all. We are done here. Thank you for your time."

"Thanks fer wastin' me time, pigs," the man said with a snarl, slamming the door.

Several minutes elapsed; then, the old man approached the clock and shifted it, releasing both fellows.

Taylor brushed the dust from his jumpsuit and asked, "Hey, you think you can get me out of these handcuffs? I don't have slippery wrists like Ferri. And do you maybe have a change of clothes?"

The old man laughed. "Ya want me to rub yer belly and make you some tea too, yer majesty?"

"I don't want to be a burden. We'll just leave," Taylor said, feeling uneasy.

The elderly man slapped his knee and let out a grimy chuckle. "I'm just yankin' yer stroodle, boy! Foller me and I'll get ya outta them shackles."

The cuffs were no match for the man's bolt-cutters. They split the metal like a stick of room-temperature butter.

Taylor cleaned the blood from his wrists and re-bandaged the cuts as best as he could. He thanked the man. "We really appreciate you helping us out like this. What's your name?"

"Hughman. Kurt Hughman," the man mumbled. "I'm glad I could help ya, boys. Ever'body deserves a second chance. I'm sure glad I got mine."

The rest of the night passed without a noise from within the small cabin.

TAYLOR WOKE THE NEXT morning just as a sliver of sunlight slipped through a crack in the wall beside him, warming his cheek. Thoughts of what might become of Ferri—and of himself—darted through his mind. He stood, changed into the clothes the old man had given him, and stepped out of the room. A quick glance back at his bloodstained prison uniform reminded him he was free from Flemett's confining grip.

'But for how long?' he thought.

The old man had left them alone in the cabin. It was unclear when he'd left. Ferri perched on the front porch railing, finishing a cigarette that he'd found somewhere.

"Got another one of those?" Taylor asked.

"Nope. It was my last one. And I don't plan on having another. Gotta clean up for my Maaryam."

"Your what?"

"My daughter," Ferri replied.

"Oh," Taylor said. He feined for a smoke, but figured it best to call it quits as well. It wasn't like he needed it outside of prison.

"You ready to roll?" Taylor asked.

36

Ferri threw the cigarette on the ground and stomped it out. Looking back at Taylor, he asked, "Whoa, did you stitch that up yourself?"

Taylor reached up towards his face. Ferri was right. The wound was expertly stitched, as if by a doctor while he slept.

"I guess Kurt did this while I was asleep. I must have been out *hard!* Where is the old coot anyhow?"

Ferri shrugged.

Taylor grabbed a pencil and paper from the old man's desk and began scribbling a thank-you note.

> Words cannot express how grateful me and Ferri are for your help last night. We are on our way West to start a new chapter in our lives. We won't forget you. Thanks for the second chance.
> -Taylor

With that, Ferri and Taylor began westward. A long journey was ahead of them, but they were happy enough to be uncuffed and out of the orange jumpsuits. Their lives were no longer restricted by the barren walls of Flemett.

Many hardships still lay ahead, and they knew it—but as they emerged from the New York forest and stepped onto the highway, they finally felt free for once.

4

ELEMENTS

___C___ FERRI AND TAYLOR had brisk-walked almost twenty-five miles before the sun began making its way down toward the horizon.

Ferri looked to his left, where Taylor was walking next to him. "We should find some shelter. If we hustle tomorrow, we can probably get to Cleveland before nightfall."

Taylor gave him an affirmative nod, and they spread out to skim the surrounding woods.

The sun soon dipped below the horizon, casting a darker shade across the land. Taylor was still within earshot, but Ferri felt alone and vulnerable in the woods, far from the city, with nightfall approaching. He pondered this as he strained his eyes in the failing light. He paused briefly to listen for Taylor, and he heard his footsteps crunching leaves probably a hundred feet to his left. Ferri pushed through the woods, moving toward the sound with haste.

Once he caught sight of a grey shirt just ahead of him, he shouted, calling him closer.

"Hey, I think we should just find a good enough spot and build a fire. It's getting colder by the minute. We're warm now because we've been keeping a solid pace, but once we stop for the night, it's gonna get chilly."

Taylor pondered this for a second. He nodded his head and immediately began breaking dead branches off of the surrounding trees.

Ferri walked just downhill of Taylor and began collecting pieces from a few fallen trees. They had thick limbs that would make good nighttime fuel for the fire. He walked back to the clearing where Taylor was now kneeling, trying to stack a pile of twigs for kindling. Ferri dropped an armload of small logs near Taylor's pile of twigs. He began kicking the leaves and brush aside, burying his foot deep enough into the ground to rip up the vegetation until he had created a five-foot fire ring.

Taylor raked some leaves with his fingers until there were enough in the middle of their circle to get a flame going without making too much smoke. They had thought little about it before, but the fire that would keep them warm tonight was also going to be a signal fire for the cops, who would still be hunting for them. He thought for a moment about how many cops might be within a few miles of them at that very moment. Pushing that thought out of his mind, he began stacking twigs onto the leaf pile.

Seeming in sync with each other, they hurried to set up a fire as the cold bit harder at their skin. Taylor pulled a lighter out of his pocket that he had swiped from the old man's cabin. The leaves were dry enough to catch fire fast. He got the small pile going in less than a minute. The flame was small, but it would do the job. Within a few more minutes, they had a fire that would provide them enough warmth to keep from freezing to death, so long as they kept up with it throughout the night.

Once there was a decent coal pit, they spread out once again to gather up enough wood for the night. Afterward, they settled back around the fire.

Pulling his arms tighter into the light jacket the old man had given to him, Taylor broke the long silence that had been lingering.

"We need to get some sleep now, but we should take shifts. I'll take the first shift. I'll wake you when it feels like two hours, and we'll alternate. Sound good?"

Ferri nodded and stretched out on the ground near the fire. He didn't argue about getting the first bit of shuteye.

VIOLENT SHAKING STIRRED FERRI from a nearly comatose state. He woke up swinging. Taylor fought hard to hold Ferri still and low.

He whispered his words. "Ferri, we have company. We have to go now. I think they've seen the fire."

Ferri looked around.

Sure enough, he saw distant trees being illuminated by flashlights. Already missing the fire, Ferri spent a few seconds as close as he could to the fire without catching his clothes. Taylor slapped his arm and brushed past him.

"We have to go now! Put out the fire!"

They kicked some earth over the fire and began moving perpendicular to the cops, in the direction they assumed to be west.

A few uneventful hours into the walk, they reached a building. It looked to be a large supply warehouse. Big rigs surrounded the place, but all was silent inside. Unsure of the human presence on the compound, the two kept as silent as possible.

Keeping to the shadows, Taylor took the lead and headed toward one of the eighteen-wheelers.

He stopped just behind the door of one of the trucks.

"I'm gonna see if it's unlocked," he said in a serious tone. "Watch my back and be prepared to fight if somebody jumps out! We can't afford to get caught by anyone right now."

Ferri shuddered at the thought, but steeled his resolve and prepared himself for anything.

Taylor pulled on the door handle.

"Locked."

Ferri led the way to the next truck. Without pause, he tested the handle of this one. A feeling of complete surprise overcame him as the handle unlatched the door.

He looked at Taylor and whispered, "Unlocked! I'll open and you get in there."

Taylor nodded and fixed his eyes on the door. Ferri yanked the door open, and Taylor was in the cab before he could exhale the breath he was holding.

"It's clear," Ferri heard Taylor say.

Taylor poked his head back out of the cab. "Come on up."

Ferri climbed into the truck. He shut the door, still on edge and being careful not to make much noise. There was a decent-sized living space in the back of the cab. Ferri noted the top and bottom bunks in the rear, but Taylor was already one step ahead, crawling into the bottom bunk.

"We should take advantage of this opportunity and sleep until morning. We should just hope that nobody is driving this truck anytime soon."

Ferri hit the locks on the doors and pulled the curtains shut that separated the living space from the front.

"Truck driving wouldn't be the worst job," he thought.

As soon as he had crawled up into the top bunk, exhaustion plowed into him like a driving wind, and he fell asleep.

THE TWO MEN WOKE a few hours later to the sound of someone pulling on the locked handle of the truck.

___Z___ A sharp tingle swept through Taylor's spine as he sat up on the bed, hackles raised.

Above him, Ferri said in a whisper, "What are we gonna do, man?"

Taylor searched the inside of the truck for something to protect himself with, being as stealthy as possible. His hand rubbed against a solid object that was stored beneath the bed, so he grabbed and pulled it out. A fire extinguisher.

Taylor looked up at Ferri, a grim expression plastered on his face. "We might have to fight. Get ready."

"We don't even know who this guy is or what he wants. What if he will drive us somewhere?" Ferri said, confused.

That sparked an idea in Frye's mind, and he went silent. He crept towards the driver's seat, hiding just behind it. Fire extinguisher raised above his head, he waited for the stranger to open it.

The next few moments dragged on for Ferri. Sitting on the upper bunk, he watched the stranger, a young man with a big coat and a ball cap, climb into the truck. He watched Taylor spring from behind the driver's seat and smack the fire extinguisher into the man's head. A heavy thunk echoed in the cramped cabin as metal collided with bone. The young truck driver slumped in the seat.

Ferri shook his head, feeling overcome with guilt. Taylor grabbed the trucker's keys and wallet and took the travel documents out of his limp hands. Then, he grunted as he drug the unconscious man out of the cab and onto the ground outside. He cranked the big rig, and his eyes watched the area in front of him with care to ensure nobody would spot them. Fortunately, no one else was present in the area. A minute later, the two pulled out of the front gate, leaving behind an unconscious man who would wake with the worst headache of his life.

The road was bumpy for a while. A bedspring made its way into Ferri's back, so he moved up to the passenger seat for a more comfortable ride. A mud-covered sign moved in and then out of view.

CLEVELAND—15 MILES

Ferri looked to his left at Taylor. His pale, blank face stared through the windshield at the road ahead.

Ferri cleared his throat. "You okay, Frye?"

Taylor's stale expression was unchanged as he responded, "You know I didn't want to do that, right?"

A few moments later, he said, "Things are different now. At any point in time, someone could catch us and drag us back to the cells that used to hold us captive. We can't take chances anymore, Ferri. We can't trust anyone but each other. It's you and me. That's it. That's all we have until this all settles down. I knocked that man out and took his things so you didn't have to. You already knocked out that guard back at Flemett. I choked out a dog. Jeez." He stared at the dashboard for a few fleeting seconds.

"We need to be better than the criminals the world thinks we are! For ourselves and for our families. We're leaving behind our old selves. Time to start fresh and do it right this time!"

Ferri agreed with a nod. Thoughts raced through his mind, but didn't seem to get anywhere. There was a traffic jam of thoughts somewhere in there, waiting at the foot of a giant wall of brainfog. The past few days felt like one endless day that kept getting stranger.

Taylor missed a gear as he shifted, causing a terrible grinding sound. He glanced at Ferri with a look that said, 'Oops!'

Ferri thought of peppering him with questions—*Where are we going? What's the plan? What do we do if we get pulled over? Do you even know how to drive something like this?*—but mental fatigue kept his tongue still. Instead, he sat back in the passenger seat and stared at the road ahead.

A few miles down the highway, Taylor let out a string of mumbled swears as he noticed lights in his rearview mirror. He smashed his fist onto the steering wheel.

"*Aww, come on!* Alright, Kamara, I'll do all the talking here, okay? My dad was a trucker, and I took trips with him all the time. I'll use the guys ID from the wallet I stole. WIth this stupid bandage on my face, he hopefully won't know the difference."

He pulled the truck onto the shoulder of the highway and put on a pair of sunglasses that the driver had left on the dashboard. Two cops got out of the cruiser behind them and approached Taylor's window.

"Well, we are out of fire extinguishers," Ferri said, trying to make light of the terrible situation.

Taylor laughed, looking at the female officer in his mirror. "I'm glad I'm out of that jumpsuit! This officer-lady is cute, and I'm pretty sure she wouldn't give me her number if I was wearing orange. That color did nothing for my complexion!"

The two shared a nervous laugh before putting on their best impressions of tired, washed-up truckers. Taylor pulled the airbrake and rolled his window down.

The male guard climbed up the steps and greeted him. "Good day, fellas. Did you know you have a taillight out?"

Taylor smiled and nodded. "Sure did! We're heading back to maintenance in Cleveland right now to get it swapped out."

The officer nodded. "Great. I've got a trainee with me today doing her first check-ride. Let me grab your license so I can show her how to run it."

Ferri felt himself tense at the question, but little did he know, Taylor was ready for this moment. He presented the actual driver's ID from the stolen wallet and gave the guard a big smile. Ferri hoped the bandage covered enough face to keep the cop from noticing the difference.

"Thanks," the officer said, looking at the picture on the ID. "There's no giant bandage in the picture on your license. I can't accept this."

Frye froze up and let out a nervous laugh.

An awkward moment of silence passed before the guard nudged his shoulder. "I'm joking, man. We will have you processed through shortly. Just hang tight while I run through the procedure with my partner. Be right back."

When the officer walked away, Ferri and Taylor glanced at each other in relief.

Ferri looked out his window at a bird perched on top of a power line. "Why don't birds get electrocuted on power lines?" he asked.

Taylor looked over and chuckled. "Why don't you ask them?"

Ferri replied with a hint of sass in his voice, "Why don't you go get the lady-cop's number instead of staring her down in your mirror?"

Taylor adjusted his sunglasses and clammed up. "Mind your own business, pretty boy."

Ferri smiled and rested his head back on the seat. He didn't feel nervous anymore. Somehow, all cares had gone out the window once the officers had walked away.

The female cop came up to the window this time and handed Taylor the license. "All looks good, sir. You two have a safe trip. Wow, what happened to your face? They let you drive this thing one-eyed like that?" She laughed.

Frye grabbed the ID and grinned. "Long story, ma'am. You take it easy."

The air released from the brakes, and the truck rolled back onto the highway.

"I need to get rid of this bandage," Taylor said, grumbling.

In the distance, Cleveland's tall buildings were visible through the smog.

Ferri turned up the radio and threw a crushed can at Taylor. "I think we are gonna be just fine."

Taylor threw the can back. "You need to start pulling your weight, sucker. It's been the Frye Show so far today, and I'm the handicapped one here!"

Ferri looked out at the setting sun. "My time will come," he said.

___C___ Six more hours passed, and finally the fuel light on the truck illuminated. Taylor pulled the rig into an old industrial park Ferri had spotted.

It was the middle of the night. Winter frost was settling on everything. This particular industrial park seemed abandoned or at least seldom used, so the two weren't particularly worried about being spotted.

They readied the cab to get some sleep before they woke up to run the truck totally out of gas.

Ferri searched for any more old water bottles lying around the cab.

"No luck. We're gonna be getting thirsty soon."

Taylor nodded in reply and peeked out a window. "Yeah, I'm not too worried about it. Looks like rain is about to come in, so we should be able to collect some rainwater in those tarps out there."

Ferri squinted to see through the glare of the cab lights. The moon provided just enough light outside to illuminate a giant tarp blowing around on the other side of the park.

"I'll set something up," Ferri said.

Ferri found a jacket balled up in the cab and put it on. He felt nothing of use in the pockets, but the thought sparked a memory of the thing from the woods that he'd stashed in his pocket while they were walking. He produced the object from his pocket.

He stared at it, unsure of what a granradurhatinator was. He fiddled with it, trying to estimate its purpose.

'If nothing else,' he thought, 'maybe it's something we can sell later.'

Stuffing it back into a pocket, Ferri emerged from the cab. The clouds were moving in and would soon cover up all the moonlight, leaving them in darkness. He moved across the lot with haste towards the flailing tarp. Someone had fastened it to the front of an old shipping container, and it was nearly coming off. Overall, it seemed to be in good shape. It was fixed at two points at the top and bottom of the left side of the container. He pulled up the tarp to free the bottom corner. Then he looked around for something to re-fasten the corners in an orientation that would allow them to collect water. He found some scrap electrical wire lying on the ground nearby and used the pieces to complete the rigging. Once the tarp was in place, he searched for a container to catch the water flowing off of the tarp.

To his left, Taylor rounded the side of the shipping container holding a five-gallon bucket. He dumped out a few nails and screws from the bottom and brushed out some residual rust.

"This should be fine," he said. "It's not the most sanitary, but beggars can't be choosers."

He placed the bucket at the point he was certain was where the water would fall from the tarp.

Ferri felt a cold drop hit his arm. "Just in time!" he said.

Briefly glancing around, he noticed that there was no lock on the shipping container. He knew it would be to their benefit to keep looking for any supplies that they might need. He pulled open the latches on the container while Taylor inspected the water-catcher one last time.

A plume of nauseating smells assaulted Ferri as he opened the door. He choked.

"Holy crap. I think something died in here."

Taylor walked closer, hiding his face in his shirt. "Yeah, that's ripe!"

Ferri stepped back away from the container briefly to take a deep breath of fresh air, then he went inside. Beer bottles and trash littered the bottom of the container. Bags of rotting trash leaned against the walls. In the back were a few crates and wooden skids. Outside, the soft patter of drops had turned into a torrential downpour.

'At least we won't thirst to death now,' Ferri thought.

Rummaging through the spoils, Ferri was able to find a canned energy drink that had yet to be opened and another lighter, but other than that, there was nothing else in the container that they could use.

"We're saved!" he said, waving the energy drink in Taylor's face. "Don't these things give you wings?"

Taylor smirked. "You wish."

The two headed out of the container and ran back to the truck. Climbing inside, they each took their places where they would sleep for the night. Taylor hugged a golf club that he'd picked up from the smelly container, just in case.

"We shouldn't have any company tonight, so let's try to catch up on sleep," Ferri said.

Taylor nodded. "Gladly!"

The two fell asleep almost immediately.

THEY AWOKE AROUND TEN o'clock the next morning to the sight of snow piled high on the hood of the truck.

DIre STraITS

5

___**Z**___ "YOU GOT A snow shovel?" Ferri asked, staring at the heaping mound of snow on the hood.

"I got this golf club," Taylor said with a snicker.

Ferri climbed down from the top bunk and exited the cab. "Well, bring that club over here and help me knock this snow off so we can get moving."

Taylor got out of the truck, and a gust of wind flung snow down the back of his shirt, sending chills down his spine. Ferri had already cleared most of the snow off by the time he started using his own inadequate tool. He pushed the last remaining clump of snow off of the truck with the nine-iron, then tucked it under his shoulder and put his hands into his pockets.

"We need warmer clothes, man. I'm freezing."

Ferri agreed with a *burrrh,* and they climbed into the truck to continue their trip. Taylor got the truck fired up and let it warm up for a few minutes before pulling out of the industrial yard and getting back on the road.

Just a few minutes down the road on the outskirts of town, the truck began beeping.

"Ah, man. Pretty much out of gas, already!" Taylor said. "I have to pull over, Ferri. We won't be able to get fuel unless you've been hiding about two-hundred bucks."

49

"What's in that guy's wallet? Anything?" Ferri asked.

Taylor's eyes lit up. He thought he'd seen a green bill of some sort poking out of it when he'd pulled out the license yesterday. He pulled the wallet out of his pocket and slid out a single, wrinkled bill.

"It's a twenty! We're rich, Ferr Bear!"

Ferri wrinkled his brow.

"What? You expected more?"

"Ferr Bear?"

Taylor giggled. "That's what came out, so that's what it's going to be! I'll use it more often now that I know you don't like it."

Ferri rolled his eyes. "Well, twenty dollars isn't worth spending on gas. Let's just park the truck and go find some food."

"Easy now," Taylor replied. "We could easily spend our whole wad on one meal! We need to be careful with this baby." He handed the money and wallet to Ferri for safekeeping while he drove to find a final parking spot.

An empty alley in the small town of Mentor, Ohio, ended up being the final pit-stop. They grabbed what little they had and started on foot. Making sure they stayed hidden, the two crept from alleyway to alleyway looking for food, water, money, or anything else that would give them hope.

"This whole escaping thing sucks," Taylor said, his mood tanking with each passing minute.

"Well, we knew what we signed up for," Ferri replied. "I'd much rather be out here hungry, thirsty, freezing, and broke than be in Flemett with no hope for a tomorrow."

Taylor chuckled. "You're quite the positive one, huh?"

"Anything else in that wallet?" Taylor asked. "Credit cards would be nice!"

They went through the wallet together. It held nothing but the man's driver's license and a picture of his pet hamster. Ferri produced the money from his pocket and cleared his throat. "We have to be smart about how we spend this. What do we need more—food, water, clothes, a disguise?"

Taylor responded with no hesitation. "*Food!* I can handle the cold, I can drink out of puddles or eat snow, and we don't need a disguise because we know better than to go out in the open. Plus, what are we going to do, buy fake mustaches?"

Ferri looked confused. "Well, if we don't go out in the open, how will we get food?"

Taylor paused for a moment, looking down the alley. "Hand me the money; I have an idea."

Ferri handed the bill over. Taylor stood up and clenched the money. He approached a homeless man who was sleeping at the end of the alley. A slight nudge was enough to wake the old man without startling him.

The man looked at Taylor and scoffed. "What the hell you want?"

Taylor stooped to talk. "Me and my friend over there, we're starving. I'm sure you are too, so I have a deal for you. Go down the street and buy us some food. I don't care what it is. You bring it back to us and you can have whatever money is left over, alright?"

The man jumped to his feet. "You got yourself a deal, son. Be back in a jiffy."

The old guy grabbed his satchel and jogged off.

Taylor returned to Ferri, a smile on his face. "He'll be back shortly with some food."

"Dude! Nice work!"

The two shared a crisp high-five.

Five hours later

"I CAN'T BELIEVE THAT guy would just take our money like that!" Taylor said, frustrated.

Ferri tried to calm Taylor down. "Maybe something happened to him. I'm sure he didn't mean to do that to us."

Taylor stood up from the cold ground, a piece of his pants ripping off after being frozen to the concrete.

"Where are you going?" Ferri asked.

Taylor didn't respond or even look back. He just continued walking onto the busy downtown street in broad daylight.

Ferri called out to him in a shouted whisper. "Frye! Wait up!"

___C___ Ferri tracked behind Taylor's heels as they wandered the streets, trying their best to blend in and look inconspicuous. On this side of town, there were fewer people around to notice them than they had expected, but they knew they couldn't be too careful.

Ferri caught the sideways glance of a young girl walking with her friends ahead of them. Taylor veered right and away from them, but Ferri felt entranced. The girl was a spitting image of Maaryam. Underneath her winter hat, he could see her shimmering black hair and bright green eyes—just like his daughter's. His eyes welled up with tears as he walked closer. He stopped to wipe the tears from his eyes.

Upon closer inspection, however, he realized the girl was not his daughter. She finally looked up and made eye contact with Ferri. Immediately, Ferri broke eye contact and turned away, realizing his mistake.

He could not afford to draw attention to himself like this. Any stranger might recognize his face from the news on the TVs that were plastered around the city. As he neared Taylor again, a hand reached back and jarred him with a slap across the head.

"Stay focused, man. What were you thinking? Were you trying to get a phone number or something?"

Ferri shook his head, embarrassed. "Sorry. I thought I saw my daughter." He felt stricken with anxiety.

Taylor grabbed his arm. "Look, man. Let's just find some food and get to someplace invisible, and then we can take a breather for a bit."

Ferri nodded.

They moved steadily through the small town, pausing in certain spots to let people pass with little notice. A man stood in front of the post office a short way ahead of them. Taylor noticed the man and slowed his pace. That man shifted focus toward them.

In a whisper, Ferri said, "He's looking right at us."

Taylor spun around and stopped facing Ferri. "Just act cool, Ferr. What's he doing?"

Ferri snuck a glance at the man. "He just threw his cigarette, and he's going back inside."

Hearing the door shut behind the man, Taylor whipped around and ran up toward the post office entrance.

"Frye!" Ferri said, again in a whisper-yell. "What are you doing?"

Taylor stopped at the door before entering. He leaned down and picked up the abandoned cigarette. He took a puff.

"Score! It's still got a cherry!" he said, excited.

Ferri rolled his eyes.

He used the cuff of his sleeve to wipe the frost from the panes of the door, then he cupped his hands to the glass and peeked inside. He stood still for a moment, staring into the window.

After a minute or so, he turned and strolled down the steps to Ferri. He handed him what was left of the cigarette. Ferri accepted it and took a big drag. He nearly coughed up a lung, reminding him why he wanted to quit.

They walked away from the post office toward a quaint little place called Annabelle's Diner. An old cream-colored Cadillac sat on the side of the building, and something inside caught Ferri's eye. He crept up to it.

Laid out on the backseat were several large grocery bags full of fresh food. He looked around, feeling his nerves spool up again. Not a soul was in sight. He checked the door handles.

'Locked.'

He stepped back from the car, shaking his head. It didn't feel right. His stomach grumbled, yet an inner feeling suggested that there was a better way.

53

Taylor caught up with him. "Yo dude! We *have* to have that. Break the window and we'll snatch it and run."

Ferri tossed the cigarette butt in a nearby trash can. "No, I have a better idea. Follow my lead."

Ferri then spun around and headed to the corner of the parking lot. He stood and waited.

Taylor looked a bit irritated. "I'm starving here, man. Why can't we just break the window and run? I'm freezing, and I bet that car has heat. We can just hot-wire it and get out of here!"

Ferri spoke without taking his eyes off the vehicle. "There are fresh groceries in there. We can only assume that the owner is just here temporarily to grab something from the diner before heading home with groceries. If I'm correct, the owner of the vehicle should be back to the vehicle anytime. When they return, follow my lead."

Taylor looked satisfied with this, for now.

Sure enough, a few minutes later, an elderly woman emerged from the diner with what appeared to be her dinner. She stopped at the driver's side and set a to-go bag on the hood.

"Move in," Ferri instructed, "and don't do anything crazy. Just follow my lead."

The woman opened the driver's side and set the to-go bag in the passenger seat. She sat down and then noticed Ferri approaching. With a look of tense curiosity, she shut the door, turned on the vehicle, and rolled the window partly down.

"Can I help you?" she asked.

Ferri replied with a charming smile. "Yes, ma'am. We are looking for a hospital. We sustained some injuries on a camping trip, and we need to have them looked at. Can you please point us in the right direction?"

She glanced back and forth between them, observing their amateur bandage-jobs. "Well, you aren't too far. It's just a couple blocks up that'a'way." She pointed to the street heading south. "But, you boys shouldn't be walking around in this cold, especially being injured. Let me give you a ride. It's not too far out of my way."

She reached back and scooted some of her groceries to the side to make room for a backseat passenger. Taylor looked at Ferri and smiled. Ferri just shrugged and opened the door to let Taylor inside.

"Why don't you sit up here next to me?" she said to Taylor, moving her diner food to the rear floorboard.

Ferri circled to the passenger side, then he got in. Taylor jumped in the back next to the groceries. Relief flooded them as the heat from the vehicle began thawing out their faces and hands. The woman began speaking about her granddaughters that she would cook for when she arrived home. As she reached for the shifter to put the car in drive, Ferri began shaking vehemently. His eyes rolled to the back of his head, and strange noises began to come from his throat.

The woman looked horrified. Taylor reached forward and clasped Ferri's shoulders.

"Hey, what's happening, man?"

Ferri spun in his seat as he convulsed toward the passenger door. Taylor studied Ferri's face with a look of concern. Ferri glanced back at Taylor and winked. The woman did not see. She was fumbling in her purse for her phone.

Taylor picked up on the unspoken cue from Ferri. "Hey, lady. I think we need some help. Can you run back into that diner and get someone? I'll keep an eye on him."

The woman opened the door in a panic and walked inside as swiftly as she could. As soon as she disappeared inside, Ferri stopped shaking and hopped into the back seat to grab some bites of food. He thought Taylor might join him in stuffing his face for a moment, but instead Taylor crawled into the front seat.

Ferri looked at him, his eyes growing wide. "Hey, T. What are you doing?"

Throwing the car in drive, Taylor sped out of the parking lot and started down the road.

"Whoa, whoa, whoa! *Wait!* This wasn't what I meant, Taylor! We can't take that poor old lady's car!"

Taylor roared with laughter. "Kamara! You're a genius! We have food *and a ride!*"

Ferri shook his head. This wasn't how he'd thought it would go.

"I just wanted a couple bites of food! I thought that would give us enough energy to figure out the next move."

Taylor sneered. "Dude, no way! That lady was coming out with reinforcements at any second. You would have been stuffing your face when she walked back out, and they'd be onto us. Even if they didn't recognize us from the news, I think it's frowned upon to trick old ladies into stealing their dinner."

"It's probably even more frowned upon to steal their cars!"

Taylor shrugged. "It's done, Kamara! Get over it. We can write her a sorry note later."

Ferri put his head in his hands. Guilt gnawed at him now much worse than the hunger.

Taylor pulled the car onto the side of the road. They were several miles out of the town and no one else was around. He got out and joined Ferri in the backseat. He laughed as he held up various half-gallons of ice cream, a gallon of milk, fresh vegetables, assorted deli meats, cheeses, and several other snack items.

"Dorothy's grandkids won't go hungry tonight. They'll figure something out, but we, my friend, we are *set!* This will last us a week."

The guilt still weighed on Ferri, but the sight of the food did perk him up a bit.

"Look, Taylor, I don't feel good about all this! But like you said, it's already done. We can't just take it all back. We might as well make it worth our while. But I really want to try harder to be a better person, you know? For my Maaryam. No more of this stealing and violent behavior!"

Taylor nodded. It seemed sincere, not like the nods he gave Ferri when he disagreed but just didn't want to argue—or just didn't care.

"Now, there's only one thing that we still need," Ferri said.

"Gas money," Taylor replied.

Ferri palmed his forehead. "I forgot about that one. So, besides gas money, we *also* need water. We forgot to get the water from the industrial park that we collected in the tarp."

Taylor shook his head. *"I didn't forget anything! The water was your job!* But it was ice this morning, anyway. We'll get some soon. Let's drink all this milk and then fill up the jug at a spigot somewhere. That will do for now."

"Gallon challenge?" Ferri said with a half-smile.

Taylor laughed. "I think not."

___Z___ WITH FULL BELLIES and a new sense of hope, the two continued driving, passing through many towns into Indiana. They knew fewer people equalled a lesser chance of getting caught. They stopped after a few hours so that Ferri could take over driving, mostly because Taylor wanted to look out the window.

"Wow. This place is barren," Taylor said, looking out at the snow-covered cornfields.

"Yeah, but I feel much more comfortable driving through here. There's only been three or four cars in the last hour."

The sun began creeping closer to the tree line in the distance, and an orange tinge filled the sky.

Before the sun left the horizon, Ferri spoke up. "I'll find a spot to park for the night."

After taking a few back-roads near a town called Delphi, a sign came into sight on the right side of the car.

DECLAN FARM

They turned onto the dirt road that led to the farm.

Taylor looked at Ferri with concern. "What are you doing? What if someone lives here?"

Ferri grinned and replied, "The mailbox was covered with a trash bag. A sure sign of abandonment, don't you think?"

"How do you know that?" Taylor asked.

Ferri just laughed and pointed ahead. "Look at this."

An old wooden bridge led the road high over a narrow stream. The bridge had seen better days.

"Let's get out and take a look," Ferri suggested. He threw the car into park and they hopped out.

The closer they got to the bridge, the more confident Taylor felt. The wood on top looked newly replaced and sturdy enough.

Taylor jumped up and down on the structure, testing its strength.

"This thing is solid, man. I say we go for it."

Ferri knelt down and tugged on a board. "I agree. If this can't hold us up, then you're really going to have to lose some weight. Let's roll."

"Hey!" Taylor said, feigning offense, but actually just happy to have someone to joke around with. He briefly imagined what it would be like if he'd been on his own out here. He shivered.

They hopped back in the car and started the crossing. The weight of the car made the bridge creak. It even felt like it swayed a little, but it held strong. Taylor looked out the window at the rocky ground far below them. He regretted it. They were higher up than he felt comfortable with.

Just as the front tires touched the dirt road on the other side, the back tires collapsed through a section of one of the boards. The sudden halt surprised the two.

"What was *that?*" Taylor said.

Ferri peered into his rearview mirror and then slammed his fist on the wheel. "We didn't check the whole bridge."

Taylor looked out the window again towards the stream.

"Oh, man. We are high up. I hope this thing holds up, or we are in for a long fall."

Ferri looked at him sideways. "Don't say that, you idiot! You'll jinx us! Just get out and see if you can get the wheels unstuck. I'll stay here and wait for your signal to pull up."

Taylor got out and began shimmying across the side of the bridge, closing his eyes and pretending he wasn't that high up. Once he got to the back of the car, he knelt down to assess the damage. Both rear tires had broken through, though not completely. It shouldn't be too difficult to get the car out if they could get traction.

"I'm gonna try to make a ramp for you, okay? Don't move the car."

Ferri held up a thumb to show he understood, and Taylor grabbed a board. The nails were loose after the breakage, so a quick tug got the wood out. He made two little ramps under the tires, hoping that would be enough to roll the car back up onto the bridge.

"Alright, Ferri, go ahead and give her some gas!"

The engine grew louder and louder, but the tires didn't want to roll.

"More! *More!*" Taylor shouted, trying to be heard over the engine.

Ferri pressed his foot to the floor, and the car jolted forward. The sudden shift in weight broke the ramps that Taylor had made and sent the back of the car straight through the wood, further breaking the boards supporting the back end. The weight began pulling the car in the wrong direction.

"Forward, now!" Taylor yelled, feeling frantic.

The back wheels spun with nothing to grab on to, and the front wheels slid backwards. The bridge underneath Taylor gave in to the pressure and broke beneath his feet, sending him careening over fifty feet straight down toward the shallow stream.

As Taylor fell, his perception of time decelerated. Mid-fall, he looked up at the bridge. The last remaining planks shattered, and chips of wood rained down like snowflakes.

The car tipped off the bridge and began following him down towards the stream. A moment later, his helpless body slammed into the rocky stream, and the car right on top of him.

___C___ FERRI HAD LOST consciousness in the collapse. He was now hanging upside down in his seat, belt fastened. Warm liquid formed droplets that fell from his head in a steady drip every other second. Blinking his eyes open, he flared his nostrils to smell as his brain tried to investigate the situation. He touched his hand to his head to feel for any irregularities. He felt what was likely a cut on top of his head. When he drew his hand away, blood covered his fingers. He knew by the smell. The headlights of the car were still on, and the surrounding snow reflected just enough light to make sight possible.

Looking just past his hand, he could make out broken glass and a stain of blood in the water that flowed gently across the roof of the vehicle from the small stream. He focused on a strange shape. His vision was still very blurry, and he knew his eyes could be deceiving him.

'Is that...a hand?'

He rubbed his eyes with the cuff of his sleeve. As the trauma of what just happened unfolded in his head, he was jolted by the realization that the hand must belong to Taylor.

He wished to be free of the vehicle, but as he looked for an escape route in a panicked state, he realized he was trapped. The entire roof of the upside-down car was caved in onto the seats in the back of the vehicle. He couldn't escape through the back seat. A large boulder obstructed the driver's-side window. The passenger side of the vehicle was compacted from the fall.

A feeling of pure manic terror came over Ferri. He snapped his head back and forth, surveying the apparent lack of options, and felt sick. He gasped for each breath, as if the oxygen had run out. Bracing himself with his left arm, he unbuckled his seatbelt with his right. He managed to spin himself into a right-side-up position. This was difficult, given the small amount of cramped space inside the vehicle.

Now, Ferri felt more claustrophobic. He tried with all of his might to force the driver's seat back, to give him slightly more room, but the ceiling had caved in too closely behind the seat.

After twenty-two minutes of near hyperventilation and failed efforts to escape, Ferri slowed his breathing and could gain a small amount of control over his erratic emotions. His rational brain came back online. He removed the headrest on his seat and placed it on the ceiling of the car, beneath him. He positioned himself to sit on top of the loose headrest, which was almost totally submerged in the stream of frigid water running through the car beneath him.

His posture restricted his movement, but he knew comfort was unattainable at present. He allowed the sound of the water flowing beneath him to bring calm to his mind. In this tranquil state, he noticed a slight movement beneath him. He didn't know where the movement came from or if anything had actually moved at all, but he kept a soft, wide gaze and focused on the area beneath him.

To his utter horror, the movement had come from Taylor's hand. It flinched and clenched every few seconds, as water flowed over it through the shattered windshield. Ferri screamed a guttural noise, and for the first time, he grabbed the hand. It felt cold and lifeless. The movement could not have been voluntary, he assumed, but more likely a posthumous jolt from a nervous system being encumbered by death.

For the first time in his life, Ferri felt truly alone and abandoned. A thick blanket of hopelessness came over Ferri, and he began to sob. The adrenaline was wearing off, and Ferri could feel the cold beginning to settle into his bones. He pulled his arms and legs in tight to his body, compressing himself within the small space left in the vehicle. He continued to cry and shiver until eventually sleep took him away.

SEVERAL HOURS PASSED. FERRI stirred in his sleep as his body tried to escape its cramped position; only, movement wasn't possible. He tried to open his eyes to figure out the problem, but his eyes would not open. They had frozen shut. Tears had welded the seams shut while he slept through the cold.

'I will die in this position. I will never open my eyes again,' he thought.

He accepted this idea, and so did his body. It had already been preparing to die. He resolved to die thinking of his daughter, Maaryam, the only light that he ever had in his life. The thought itself seemed to bring him temporary warmth.

Just before he drifted into a cold sleep once more, the air trembled and a strange flash of light pierced through Ferri's eyelids. He shook off the cold with a jolt of adrenaline and rubbed his eyes until he could blink them open. Then, he looked around to decipher the situation. He caught a sliver of human conversation outside the car, partially drowned out by the sound of the stream.

A man spoke. "...ing to the tracker...anGran should be right...ont of us."

A moment later, Ferri clearly heard a second man say, "Jimmy, there's someone in there!"

THE VISITORS

6

___Z___ FERRI REACHED HIS hand out of a small opening between the car and the water to alert his potential rescuers. "Help! Please, I'm trapped!"

The two men on the outside ran around the mangled wreck and crouched down next to the driver's side to find Ferri. Only a thin sheet of metal and some plastic separated him from freedom. The car's headlights had gone out while Ferri slept.

One man outside yelled to Ferri. "We are gonna get you out, okay? Just give us a moment to think of something. My name is Jimmy. What's yours?"

"I'm Ferri," he said, his mouth struggling to move properly in the cold. "And Taylor, he...he....I think he might be dead. He's under the car."

Jimmy grabbed his partner's sleeve. "Gary! Go around and check on his friend."

Gary got up to search around the car. In the dim light of the moon overhead, he noticed a shoe lying in the stream. He circled around to the hood of the vehicle. The sight stopped his breath in his chest.

Gary had seen his fair share of gore in The Great Battle against the Boral and the Leech army, but the sight in front of him made him tremble. He shouted to Jimmy and Ferri. "I see... I see some legs...your friend's legs...and...they are no longer attached to the rest of his body. *Jimmy, get over here!*"

Jimmy hurried to observe the scene. His jaw dropped.

"Mother of God!" he said, barely audible over the running stream.

A muffled voice came from inside the car. "What? What is it?"

Jimmy knelt down and covered his eyes. "Hey, guy...uh...Ferri...is that your name? Um...we found your buddy's legs...Taylor, is it? Just hang tight. We are going to try to get to him."

Ferri tilted his head to rest on the seat. The stress of the day, the trauma of the accident, and the shivering from the past few hours had taken a toll on his body. He noticed for the first time a small, waterlogged bag next to him in the wreck.

'The grandma's diner food,' he thought. Guilt radiated through his trembling body. *'This is just karma paying us back.'*

Jimmy and Gary continued to assess the situation outside. They decided to try to lift the front of the vehicle together and slide Taylor's upper half of his body out from underneath. The weight of the car paled compared to the weight of the situation. Almost solely reliant on Gary's Leech strength, they got the front of the car in the air, and Jimmy let go to reach down and grab Taylor. Gary's legs shook. All the weight was now his to bear.

Jimmy surveyed under the car. Surprisingly, there were enough rocks under the hood to suspend the car and keep it from completely crushing Taylor's upper body. Jimmy grabbed Taylor's arm and drug him from underneath the wreck. He checked for vital signs. A thin pulse and labored breath proved true what they thought was impossible. Taylor was *alive!* Hardly, but still so.

Unfortunately, Gary and Jimmy hadn't thought of what they were going to do to help Taylor once they grabbed him from underneath the vehicle. The very instant Taylor's midsection shifted, a stream of blood and entrails began pouring out of his abdomen. In a frantic state, Jimmy and Gary began ripping pieces of their clothes off to keep the gore under control as much as possible. It proved to be too much for them to subdue.

"**Blowtorch**," Jimmy said commandingly. A blowtorch appeared in his right hand, and he motioned towards Gary. "Grab that piece of metal over there and set it in front of me."

Gary trudged through a shallow section of the stream and grabbed a quarter panel that was dislodged from the car on impact. He set it down, and Jimmy put the torch to it.

Slowly but surely, it heated. About a minute went by. Taylor still lay in the water, now unconscious, the river turning red all around him.

"Alright, Gary. The metal is hot enough," Jimmy said.

Gary turned towards Jimmy, a concerned look in his eyes. He knew what had to be done. Gary grabbed Taylor's arms and drug him to the bank of the river, where Jimmy now stood with the piece of heated metal at his feet.

Supporting him under the shoulders, Jimmy and Gary lifted Taylor's limp stub of a body onto the scorching metal. An eerie sound filled the air, one of meat sizzling. Taylor's screams soon drowned out the sound. Smoke rose as the pools of blood dripping from Taylor boiled and the exposed flesh and vessels cauterized. He lost consciousness again a few moments later.

After the major wound had sealed up, they cauterized the stump that used to have a hand attached and put one of Taylor's own socks over it. They wrapped Taylor in whatever clean clothing they had left and laid him on a dry patch of grass.

"Let's hurry and help this other guy so we can get out of here," Jimmy said, cleaning his hands in the blood-polluted water.

They extracted Ferri more rapidly than they had Taylor. Ferri was able to slide himself out of the wreck after Gary lifted it. He was mostly uninjured. He grabbed Taylor's severed left hand before he exited the destroyed vehicle.

As soon as he was free, Ferri rushed over to Taylor and took a knee beside his mangled body. It was still hard to imagine him surviving his injuries. He stood up and turned to the two mystery men who had saved him.

"Who are you guys? Where did you come from?"

Jimmy walked over and put his hand on Ferri's shoulder. "We will discuss all of that soon. First, we must get your friend some help. He won't last much longer in his current state."

Just as Jimmy finished his sentence, the air by the treeline behind them warped, and a sharp but muffled buzzing rushed into Ferri's ears. He put his hand up to shield his eyes from the cornea-splitting light that emitted from the wobbling gas-like portal in front of him. He felt a change in the air pressure, and his ears popped in response. Then, a woman jumped out of the portal, dirt kicking up as she landed in a superhero-like pose.

"What on *Earth* is going on right now?! Can someone *please* explain any of this to me?!" Ferri said.

Jimmy and Gary walked over to embrace Siiva, their friend from across the galaxy. Siiva walked towards Taylor with a purpose, not acknowledging Jimmy and Gary's attempt at greeting her, or their partial nudity.

Siiva pointed a demanding finger at Ferri.

"Keep it cool, human. Every one of you always has to have a hissy fit whenever you see someone teleport for the first time." She turned to Jimmy. "Put him on my back so I can get him some real help. Your feeble attempts won't be able to save his life, but Dr. Bann can help."

Mere seconds later, the men had Taylor's upper-half mounted on Siiva's back, and she swept away into another portal, Taylor in tow.

Ferri stood in a puddle of his friend's blood. He couldn't wrap his mind around anything that had happened in the last few hours. Dropping to a knee, he felt enveloped in a warm, fuzzy haze. His eyes closed involuntarily. He began to feel strangely...better.

A muffled voice said, "Gary, I told you not to use that mind-numbing power yet! There's no telling what memories you could erase. Let's get back to Jopulous before Siiva rats us out. We are already going to be in big trouble with the Ardent for getting involved in all of this. Find GranGran. It's on this guy somewhere. Oh, don't forget that guy's hand. He can still have it re-attached if we hurry."

TAYLOR OPENED HIS EYES and looked at the ceiling above him. There was an aquarium built into it. He watched small blue fish swim around for a few seconds before his mind sprang into action.

He sat upright on his bed, viewing the room. It felt like something out of a sci-fi movie. Medical technology way ahead of his time lined the walls. A tiny robot floated beside him.

Taylor turned to the robot, and just as he looked into what he assumed was an eye, the robot shouted at him. "You should not be awake yet; my results were ninety-nine percent correct that you would be in a coma for three more years."

Taylor's heart pounded. He ripped off the sheets that covered his legs, exposing his shiny new limbs. He looked at the robot, which seemed to be recalculating, its robot eyes crossing in a strange way.

"Say hello to the one percent, beeotch!"

The door to his room opened, and Dr. Bann, Gary, Jimmy, and Siiva entered, wearing smiles. Jimmy, Gary, and Siiva stood off to the side and spoke softly among themselves.

___C___ Dr. Bann reached out to shake Taylor's hand. Taylor looked at the hand, which had six fingers, and tried to figure out how to shake it. He thought of the six-fingered man from *The Princess Bride* and laughed.

"Forget it," Dr. Bann said, pulling his hand back. "How do you feel?"

Taylor cleared his throat and tried to speak but coughed instead. His vocal cords felt dusty, like an old forgotten coat in the back of the closet.

"Do you know where you are?" Dr. Bann asked.

Taylor shook his head.

"You're in Jopulous."

Taylor looked at the doctor, confused. "Is that in China or something?"

A voice behind him laughed. "We're not on Earth, ya big dummy."

The voice belonged to Ferri. Taylor spun to look at him. The Bangladeshi's black hair had grown quite a bit since Taylor had seen him last.

"How long have I been here?" Taylor asked, afraid of the answer. He added, "And how long have you been standing behind me?"

Ferri smirked.

Dr. Bann replied, "Taylor, you've been here for eighteen months, but luckily for you, only a few days have passed on your planet, so you haven't missed much back home."

'Eighteen months?!'

Taylor thought about that for a second. "Yeah, nothing to miss back there." He was unsure whether he was in total shock or just taking this new information very well.

Ferri handed Taylor a tablet. Holograms displayed different bits of information about the current state of Earth and some other major planets in the galaxy. He clicked on the hologram of Earth.

"You can talk to it if you'd like," Dr. Bann said.

Taylor looked at him sideways. "And what do I say?"

"Whatever you like."

Taylor rubbed his eyes and set the tablet down, dissolving the hologram. Now, the overwhelm was beginning to set it.

"Look. This is too much right now. Can you guys leave and let me process all of this? This is some heavy stuff, man!" he said, looking at Ferri.

"No biggie, T," Ferri said, raising his hands. "Holler if you need me."

Gary and Jimmy gave a nod to Taylor and then left the room as he requested.

Siiva ignored the request and pulled up the doctor's chair next to the Taylor. She eyed him with an expression that he couldn't interpret.

"Uhhh...hi. Who are you?" Taylor asked.

The woman's pale skin creeped him out. Taylor wondered if she'd ever seen the sunlight in her life.

"You're lucky to be alive!" she said. "Most humans are weak. Excessive blood loss makes your kind die quickly. You held on longer than most."

Taylor wasn't sure whether he should thank her or feel offended.

"Are you my nurse or something? I need to know before I start to feel overly creeped out. My brain is too tired to handle all this."

Siiva smiled and chuckled. "I'm Siiva. I'm not your nurse."

Taylor huffed. "Okay, if you're not my nurse, then I'd like you to leave like everybody else. I'm feeling pretty overstimula—"

"I was human once, like you," Siiva said, interrupting him.

Taylor sat with his back against the wall on his bed. He listened.

"My parents moved me to this planet when I was a little girl. Jopulous is full of many wonders. I hope you get to see at least a few of them before you leave."

Taylor stared at her, curious. "Are you from Earth then?"

"No, Earth isn't the only planet on which humans live, you know? My planet was quite advanced. My parents left to seek a simpler life. I have little memory of my old world."

"So...you *were* human? But you're not anymore?" Taylor asked.

"I'm half human. I became half-Vedren when my parents took me to meet the Core."

"I don't know what that means, but that's cool."

Siiva smiled. "Check out the tablet after I leave." She nodded toward the tablet that Ferri had left for him. "It will tell you all about it. How are your new limbs feeling?"

Taylor wiggled his toes, which—though robotic—felt to him just like his old fleshy extremities.

"They feel pretty good," he replied. "I guess I'm mostly just feeling weird about missing so much time. Eighteen months is a long time to miss!"

Siiva nodded. "It is, and it isn't. You didn't miss much, though."

Taylor grunted, moving the fingers on his reattached hand. Turning his wrist over, a hologram popped out, showing him the current time.

"Sick! Kamara's going to be jealous about this one!" He looked at Siiva, who manifested a glass of water into her hand and handed it to him.

"Whoa! That was cool. How did you do that?"

Siiva laughed. "Cerebral Solid Creation—just one of the many gifts of being a Hudren. The power of CSC usually requires that the item to be manifested be named, but once the process is mastered, a mental command can suffice."

Taylor's eyes widened and then fluttered. He shook his head. "Do you have other powers?"

"A few."

"What's the coolest one?" Taylor asked.

Siiva eyed him with a narrow gaze and a half smile. After a moment, she leaned forward and whispered. "Before my mother died, she gave me a gift—a secret elemental weapon. I can command the lightning itself and hold its power in my grasp, bending it to my will."

Taylor nearly drooled on himself. "That is wicked cool!"

"Unfortunately," Siiva said, sitting up and dropping the whisper, "the effect is short-lived. It's more of an emergency weapon than a power that I could summon whenever I wish. In truth, I may never get the chance to use it. Time will tell."

"Well, either way, that sounds pretty cool."

Siiva patted him on the shoulder. "Drink that water and get some rest. But if you're not too tired just yet, check out that tablet."

With that, she departed.

The room was empty a moment later, except for Taylor. He was still getting used to the feeling of being inside his body again. He had already forgotten about his new legs. They felt identical to his legs before they were severed. The attachment points were seamless, as if the legs had grown onto his body.

He picked up the tablet again. "What can you tell me?" he asked.

It replied, "What would you like to know?"

"Everything," Taylor said.

"No, you don't."

"Fine," he said. "Then what can you tell me about this place and how I got here?"

"That's more like it," the tablet replied.

For the rest of the night, Taylor listened to the intelligent tablet tell him about the wonders of Jopulous and the recent galactic struggles. He learned more about Jimmy, Gary, and Siiva, who had brought him to this new and strange place. He fell asleep feeling completely exhausted, but conveniently up-to-speed with everything that had recently happened.

THE GREEN SKULLS

7

TAYLOR AWOKE THE NEXT morning to a very large bug creature wheeling breakfast toward him.

"You've been on the medical juice for a while, so we are -oin- to have to ease you into re-ular food," the thing said.

Taylor looked at the giant bug with disgust. "What are you, and why are you not saying the letter 'g'? Are you messing with me?"

The creature looked at him through its million shimmering eyes. "I am Nurii-nar. I am the caretaker of the sacred Jopulous -ardens. Almost all the plants in the observable universe are present there. The -ardens take up three theks, or over five thousand square miles on your planet. But, there is more to the -ardens than meets the eye." He used all of his arms to point down.

Taylor looked confused.

Nuriignar pointed down more intensely.

"Down?" Taylor asked.

The bug creature nodded his head. "Yes, under-round."

Taylor narrowed his eyes. "Do you mean underground?"

The bug man nodded. "I apolo-ize, but I am physically incapable of pronouncin- the sound of that letter."

72

He pulled Taylor close to his cold, slimy chest. Taylor went limp.

Moments later, it released its grip on him, and Taylor pulled away with a gasp.

"Holy crap! You just hacked my brain! I know how to get around this entire planet now. I can't believe it!"

His stomach grumbled, and his astonished attention redirected to the magnificent breakfast that Nuriignar had rolled in. He shoveled handfuls of food into his mouth, unsure of what anything was. It all looked so bizarre, but everything tasted phenomenal. He looked up to thank the bug creature, but it had already left.

He was just finishing the food when Dr. Bann returned.

"It looks like everything is ready for your release. However, there are a few things that I would like to discuss with you first." He manifested a stool next to Taylor and sat on it. "I trust that most of your questions have been answered, so I will explain where we will go from here."

Taylor sat up, nervous.

"You and your friend, Ferri, will be escorted back to your planet tomorrow morning. You will have today to explore Jopulous, if you wish. We will discuss your return tonight before the Council. The Ardent desires to speak with you, now that you are well."

"Who is the Ardent again?" Taylor asked.

"He is the Protector of the Observable Universe."

"Jeez, that's quite the job title," Taylor said, scratching his brow. He looked at his newly reattached hand. "Did you do this too?" he asked.

Dr. Bann nodded. "Yes, but—just so it doesn't come as a surprise—the previous owner of this hand was a serial killer, so you might want to keep an eye on it, in case it gets a little...stabby."

Taylor glanced back and forth from Dr. Bann to the hand a few times, nervous sweat beading up on his forehead.

Dr. Bann cracked the air with laughter. "It was a joke. That is *clearly* your hand. But what do I know? You might just be a serial killer. Are you?" he asked with a smile.

"Actually, I am," Taylor said, maintaining fierce eye contact.

Now, it was Dr. Bann's turn to be nervous.

This time Taylor laughed. "I'm joking. I'm not that twisted. Or...am I?"

Dr. Bann put on a serious expression, looking fed up with all the joking. He stood up. "I've got some testing to get back to. Your friends should be back soon to help you out."

Taylor grabbed the remote control for his bed and tilted it back slightly. A quick nap was in order.

FERRI SAT IN GARY'S Corner, the pub that was all the hype in Jopulous these days. Gary, the pub's namesake, sat at the bar behind Ferri, buying drinks for anyone with a face. In front of Ferri sat Jimmy and Siiva, who were both arguing about something he couldn't understand. He massaged his temples and closed his eyes.

For the past few months, they had been living in this fantasy land, drinking JopHops and Leech's Bane. This was his first sober day in many months. Thoughts flooded his mind that he had been trying to ignore. Visions of his daughter, now millions of light-years away. The guard that he had injured to escape imprisonment. It all seemed like another lifetime ago, but he knew that this current reality would not last much longer.

They were going back to Earth soon. What were they going to do now? He had been told that they would meet with the Council of the Ardent tonight to discuss how best to handle the situation. He hoped that something positive would result from the meeting.

Feeling emotionally calloused and mentally adrift, he looked around the pub. Something had changed. Seconds before everyone had been clinking their gourds together in toast. Now they were all staring at him, wearing serious and even fearful expressions.

Puzzled, he looked to Jimmy and Siiva. They turned and took shocking notice of him just as a cold, metal blade kissed his Adam's apple.

___Z___ Ferri's heart stopped. He could feel the fear flowing through his body like poison squeezing its way through his congealing bloodstream. The vibrant pub had frozen in surprise, all the intoxicated patrons converging their attention on this tense scene.

Jimmy and Siiva scooted their stools out from underneath them, the scraping of wood against the floor breaking the silence. They crept towards Ferri, keeping their eyes locked onto the blade in case it moved.

Unable to tell exactly who wielded the blade, Jimmy tried to ease the tension in the room. "Okay, okay. Apparently, you, sir, aren't in a good mood. What can I do for you?"

The mysterious figure remained still and silent, but as Jimmy got closer and closer, so did the blade to Ferri's throat. Ferri swallowed what he assumed to be his last bit of hope for escaping. The blade pressed gently into his skin, drawing a small amount of blood that slowly inched down his neck before getting soaked up by his shirt collar.

About two minutes had passed since the man unsheathed his weapon. Enough time for Gary—known for his sneakiness—to slide out of the pub and alert the Jopulous Guard. Ferri watched him slip out unseen. Jimmy—Ferri assumed—knew that all he had to do was stall for a little while longer.

Jimmy grabbed a drink that sat on the counter and took a long swig. Wiping his mouth of dribble, he offered Ferri's assailant a drink.

No response.

The man was unyielding; unwavering in his intent, whatever it was.

'A little too unwavering,' Ferri thought. The guy had hardly moved this entire time.

Ferri noticed Jimmy's brow furrow as he stared at the assailant. He began waving his arms about, trying to get some sort of response out of the man.

Just then, the doors to the pub burst open, and the Jopulous Guard stormed inside, with Gary hot on their tails. They shot the perp in the back with a stun-beam, but nothing happened.

Two, three, four more beams were launched into the man in varying locations, but still not a single movement.

"Impossible," said one guardsman.

Ferri inched his hand up and grabbed the blade that rested on his throat. He yanked as hard as he could. The ease with which he was able to remove the blade surprised him. He jumped up from his stool as the stiff body of the mystery man fell face-first onto the cold floor. He felt blood trickle down his hand where he'd grabbed the blade.

The guards rushed in and flipped the body over. Right after touching it, the skin began to crack and disintegrate. All that remained was a tattered robe lying on the ground. The letters—G.S.—emblazoned the chest of the robe. The guards stood up, their faces pale as winter.

"We must alert the Ardent now!" one guard stated.

They ran out of the pub and headed straight for the Dome, leaving everyone in the pub shocked and confused.

Gary rushed over to check on Ferri, who was still a little shaken.

Jimmy turned towards Siiva. "Any idea what that 'G.S.' means?"

Siiva gave Jimmy a defeated look and motioned for him to follow her. Jimmy turned to Gary and said, "Take care of Ferri. We'll be right back." Then, he exited with Siiva to discover what on Jopulous was happening.

SIIVA AND JIMMY WALKED around to a small alleyway between the pub and the produce shop, aptly called *Nurri-nar's -lorious -roceries.*

"Jimmy, there are a few things that we have all kept from you and your partner. This info has been withheld because the Council believed the issue had been resolved, but obviously after what I've just seen, it is still very much a problem. I must notify the Council at once."

Jimmy's lips drew into a line, and his eyebrows raised. "What is it, Siiv?"

"I want you to get back to Gary and stay in the Ardent's bunker for the night. You are not safe. I'm assuming that they came for Ferri because you saved his life when he was supposed to die. Seems strange to me they came for Ferri and not Taylor, but they would know better than I. That's their job. I will have guards check on Taylor as well, but you and Gary need to hide now!"

Jimmy shivered. The air seemed to thicken with each breath. The normally vibrant color in Siiva's eyes had faded, and she was acting out of character. Almost as if she were...afraid.

He grabbed her hand. "Siiv, who are they?"

A strong pulse of energy jolted Jimmy's mind as Siiva forced words into his awareness.

'The Green Skulls. They come to balance all that has been changed, to restore order. To right others' wrongs and keep the timeline in its correct sequence. They used to have the right intentions, but they were bested by their own power and need for control. Now, they only use their power to further their own agenda.'

Jimmy opened his eyes. Siiva was gone, and so was the connection between their thoughts.

He shuddered, looking around as if he were being surveyed. This was not his first encounter with the malevolent Green Skulls.

He rushed back to the pub to grab Gary and Ferri and check on Taylor. He opened the door of the pub and stared at the room before him.

Not a single person remained. Even the furniture had vanished. The empty building had a cold breeze blowing through it.

Jimmy noticed a paper tumbling across the floor. He gathered the note and unwrinkled it.

BE BRAVE, BE OBSERVANT

FOR WHAT COMES NEXT.

YOU MESS WITH THE PAST,

YOU MESS WITH THE PRESENT.

YOU FIX COMPLEX THINGS WITH
A SIMPLE SUTURE.

BUT WHO CAN SAVE YOU IF WE
MESS WITH THE FUTURE?

G.S.

___C___ Jimmy stared at the note. He noticed that his hand was quivering and his pulse had sped up. Unsure of how to interpret the empty pub, he exited and made his way toward the Dome of the Ardent. He comforted

himself with thoughts of the Ardent making sense of everything and returning it all back to normal.

When he arrived at the entrance to the Dome, he realized the guards
were not at their usual post outside the massive doors.

'They must be inside,' he thought.

He pushed on the leftmost door to let himself inside. It didn't budge. He
tried the right door.

Nothing.

In a fit of desperation, he shoulder-checked the door.

It budged slightly.

He pushed again with all his might. The door creaked open. It was at
this moment that he realized exactly how heavy the doors were. The guards
were clearly stronger than he gave them credit for.

He continued pushing until he was purple in the face and felt like his
eyes might pop out of his head if he exerted himself more. Once the door was
open enough to squeeze through, he wriggled in through the small opening.
Looking around, it didn't take him long to realize that something was terribly
wrong. His throat constricted, stopping his breath.

Just like the pub, the Dome was empty. Jimmy panicked.

Before his emotions got the best of him, he closed his eyes and took
a few deep breaths. He knew he needed to keep it together and search for
something that would allow his mind to find any clues to the situation.

Only slightly calmer now, he checked the rear of the Dome to make
certain that there was no one there. He sat down on a long bench near the rear
of the Dome. Once again, he closed his eyes and attempted to concentrate
his thoughts.

With no one and nothing here to help him, he decided to teleport to the
Void and ask for help from The Core.

Eyes still closed, he imagined where he wanted to go and felt himself
shift into another dimension.

Only...he didn't.

When he opened his eyes, Jimmy realized he had not left the bench in the Dome. He tried again, a little more desperately.

Still nothing.

Now began the actual panic. He lost control of his breath, which was now entering and leaving his body in quick bursts. In the grip of a panic attack, unable to steady his body or mind, he collapsed onto the floor. The cold stone offered him no comfort. He continued in this fit until his weary mind drifted out of consciousness.

GARY AND FERRI HAD spent some time in the pub processing recent events. Ferri had finally calmed down after a few shots of Leech's Bane, one of the stronger liquid encouragements in Jopulous.

Breaking the silence that had been lingering for a few drinks now, Gary spoke up. "Are you doing okay, Ferri?"

Ferri stirred and looked around. "I'm not really sure how I feel, but I definitely wouldn't say that 'okay' is the word I would use. I'm tired and confused and scared, and I almost wish that I was back at Flemett. At least that place was mostly predictable."

Gary considered that before responding. He was quite worried about his friend.

"Look, I know the situation isn't ideal, but I'm sure that the Council will have it all figured out soon enough. Let's go check on Taylor and then see if we can find Jimmy before the big meeting tonight."

Ferri nodded in solemn agreement.

They slipped out of the pub and headed for the hospital where Taylor was staying.

As they walked, they talked among themselves about the beauty of Jopulous. It seemed especially quiet today. Even the birds seemed to be hiding.

They arrived at the hospital minutes later.

Opening the front door, Gary could feel that something was wrong. The inside of the building looked empty. The two of them hastened to the room where they had left Taylor. To their dismay, that room was also empty. Not even the table that Taylor had been lying on remained.

"I don't understand," Gary said, quite bewildered. An internal alarm sounded in the back of his mind. He was grateful that Ferri couldn't hear it.

Ferri sighed. "What is going on? Where is everything? And everyone? Where the heck is Taylor? *Hello!*"

He yelled again and again, but the only returning sounds were his own echoes reverberating off of the walls.

Gary exhaled in fearful frustration. "We need to get to the Dome and find Jimmy. This is all so weird."

The two of them walked back to the entrance and pulled the door open.

Neither moved another inch. Even their blood seemed frozen in place. They looked out into a dense green fog. Gary's chest felt tight. There was a smell in the air that he hadn't sensed in a long time.

___Z___ JIMMY GOT UP from the stone floor and sprinted towards the entrance of the Dome. He threw his body against the heavy doors and heaved them open again. A stiff wind and a hard reality smacked him in the face.

The once pristine vista that was usually seen upon exiting the Dome hid behind a thick, green fog that now enveloped the entire city of Jopulous.

Jimmy felt faint. He ran over to the Gardens to get some water, but a dark sludge that moved at the pace of a snail had replaced the clean water.

His heart threatened to leap out of his chest.

Jimmy scanned the city. Nothing stirred.

'It's like the city is under some sort of spell!'

He walked towards the Library in search of anything familiar.

Eventually, Jimmy spotted a strange silhouette in the distance. Where the Ardent's tall, golden statue used to stand, a smaller, frail statue now took its place. Jimmy approached the statue to investigate. It's smooth black stone hummed steadily, singing with a dark tone.

The statue was of an elderly man—not one that Jimmy recognized. Its hands clasped a scroll, unrolled and pointed outward to be read by onlookers. Jimmy got closer and tried to make out the writing. The script was indecipherable. He placed his hand on the statue's arm, and a jolt of energy hurled him back twenty feet.

"HE NOW HAS THE Mark," Marguz Phenix said, handing the Eye of the Skulls back over to his mage.

"We must act now while their city is under my spell, Marguz," said the mage.

Marguz turned to him and nodded.

The mage—Grascut, as the Skulls knew him—proceeded down the hall to his laboratory. He put the Eye on his desk, placed his hands over the glowing orb, and spoke an incantation: "Metis numil lon juolpi, nyui frity renrum dresop fecriti."

The message sent. Jopulous was vulnerable, and the Skulls were on their way. They knew the city housed the Time Keeper and his posse. The Skulls wanted to put an end to their so-called "heroics" before the naïve travelers completed their ultimate goal—preventing the assassination of Abraham Lincoln.

GARY AND FERRI MOVED outside into the foggy city. Gary felt a sharp pain in his head as he and Ferri began approaching the Dome. A voice accompanied it; Jimmy's voice. It directed him to come to the Library. They moved toward it, obeying the directive.

Upon arrival, a sight awaited them that was almost too grotesque to handle. A smaller, dark statue replaced the Ardent's magnificent statue. In front of that were three decapitated heads, mounted on stakes and covered with bags to hide all identifying features.

Ferri walked towards the heads, his hands trembling and his heart murmuring. He grabbed the bag that covered the first head and peeled it off, revealing the face of Siiva.

Gary gasped and fell to his knees. Ferri, numb from shock, moved over to the next one and removed the covering.

The Ardent's head appeared as the bag lifted, his glowing crown still perched atop his head.

Ferri threw the bag in the dirt and stared at the third head. It stood a short distance beyond the others. Ferri proceeded over to it and grabbed the bag.

Just before he pulled it off, Gary stopped him.

"I'll do it," Gary said, voice catching in his throat.

Ferri backed up and looked around at the foggy city. Gary removed the bag from the head and stared into the eyes of the final victim of the Skulls.

The head belonged to his best friend, Jimmy Truffle.

The blood drained from Gary's face, and he fell backwards onto the ground. In absolute disarray, he stumbled toward the head, noticing a note that poked out of his mouth. He gently pried open Jimmy's mouth and removed the blood-soaked paper. Unrolling it, he read:

> We did this so you could see the conse-
> quences. The fate of the universe is to
> be left unchanged, and all who attempt
> to alter our timeline must pay with
> blood. We hope this warning is enough
> for you, reader, to see that what's done
> cannot be undone. We hope never to
> deal with you again, but know that if we
> have to, it will be the last time. -Marguz
> Phenix, Head of the Green Skulls.

Immediately upon reading the last word of the note, a powerful blow struck Gary in the chest. He dropped the note and clenched his chest, unable to breathe.

Ferri reached down to pick up the note. Gary's hand swatted it out of his grasp.

"What's your deal?" Ferri said.

Gary held up a finger, gesturing for Ferri to wait a moment. He caught his breath back moments later. Through labored breaths he said, "Don't read the note. I feel something has happened to me."

GRASCUT TURNED TO MARGUZ Phenix, Leader of the Skulls, and smiled. "The other one has been marked as well, Marguz."

THE OWL

8

One hour earlier

BACK IN THE JOPULOUS hospital, a rude shake interrupted Taylor's nap. Confused and flustered, Taylor sat up and shielded his eyes to better see what was happening.

Dr. Bann hovered less than a foot from his face.

"Sorry to wake you, but we have some problems. Looks like your stay is up. Maybe mine as well. I'm afraid I have no idea what is going on. We need to find someone who does."

Taylor felt his confusion worsening. "What are you talking about? What problems? Where are we going?"

Dr. Bann offered him an arm for assistance, and Taylor stepped off of his bed to use his new legs for the first time. Once both feet touched down on the ground, he weighted his legs and attempted to straighten into standing. It worked much more easily than he had expected. In fact, it was as if his lower body had never taken a day off.

"Holy smokes, dude! These legs are killer!"

Dr. Bann grimaced. "Actually, they are completely harmless unless you direct them otherwise. I assure you."

Taylor decided against responding.

85

They walked toward the windows in the front lobby.

Outside the hospital was a bleak scene. Dense green fog blanketed everything, appearing much like smoke from a plastic fire. There wasn't a soul in sight.

Dr. Bann broke the silence after a few moments. "I looked around while you slept. I can't find anyone else. This weather is extremely unusual on Jopulous. Never in my lifetime has it happened before. There is something strange going on. My computer equipment shows an incongruity with reality on Jopulous. Things are not as they seem."

"We should go to the Dome and ask the Ardent," Taylor said.

Dr. Bann exhaled, "The Ardent is not in the Dome, Taylor. Jopulous is deserted. I can feel the lack of souls among us."

"Well, that doesn't make sense!" Taylor said in a yell. "Where would they all go?"

Dr. Bann put his hands on Taylor's shoulders, causing Taylor to flinch and pull back in distrust.

"Taylor Frye, I don't know any more than you. Let's keep our heads together."

Taylor nodded.

Dr. Bann pushed the hospital doors open, and they exited into the bleak city.

GARY SAT CRYING ON the ground in front of the heads as he had been for the past few hours. Ferri paced behind him, afraid.

"What are we supposed to do now?!"

Gary responded only with blubbering sobs.

"Hey! *Knock it off,*" Ferri said, frustrated. "We have to get it together. Do you think any of them would have wanted us to sit here and boo-hoo about it forever? It sucks! They are dead. But we need to think about ourselves now, and...Taylor! We forgot about Taylor!"

He grabbed Gary's arm and tugged him upwards.

Gary shrugged him off.

"Gary, come on. Let's go get Taylor so we can have another brain to figure this mess out."

Gary waved him off without looking up from the ground. "Leave me. I'll catch up with you."

Ferri grabbed him by the arm again. "I'm not leaving you, so come on."

In an instant, Gary sprung up, spun around, and Leech arms exploded out from his torso in a surprising transformation. Ferri fell backward, terrified. Gary relaxed and quickly returned to normal form.

Ferri recovered and tightened his brow. "I guess I'll just go it alone then."

With that, he walked away, leaving Gary with the silent heads.

Gary knelt back down on the ground, staring at the pebbles beneath him and the trickles of blood spilling into the cracks in the ground. He felt as if he had no more tears to cry. He looked up at the heads, which stared back at him with ghostly blank expressions.

"What have we done, Jimmy?" he said, voice grave.

___Z___ FERRI RAN THROUGH the city. The fog was so thick that it felt almost like walking underwater. Breathing was just as difficult.

Eventually, he heard voices in the distance and turned to face them. Taylor and Dr. Bann emerged from the fog.

"Ferri? Is that you?" Taylor said.

Ferri ran over to the two and hunched over to catch his breath.

Taylor placed his hand on Ferri's shoulder. "What is going on here, man? Are you okay?"

Ferri looked up at Taylor, his hopeless eyes answering the question for him. He cleared his throat. "We need to get to Gary. He needs our help."

After a few minutes, they arrived at the horrid scene, where the heads of their friends loomed on stakes like trophies of war. They couldn't bear to stay too long near this deathly display.

"Jopulous is too much right now. We need a safe place away from the city to recover and come up with a new plan," Ferri said to Taylor and the doctor.

Gary remained on the ground, asleep from exhaustion. Taylor scooped him up and placed him on his shoulders.

Dr. Bann opened a portal to somewhere on Earth, and the three stepped into it.

Just before it closed, a small voice called out from somewhere nearby. "Hey -uys, wait for me!"

Dr. Bann held the portal open as Nuriignar climbed out of a bush near the Library.

"Room for one more?" the bug-man asked.

Dr. Bann nodded, and Nuriignar waddled his way into the portal.

They exited the portal on the other side and stepped into a cozy cabin that was familiar to no one. Taxidermied animals adorned almost every wall. A fire burned in a stone hearth on the far wall.

"Owls are probably my favorite creatures," Dr. Bann said with excitement, looking at a stuffed owl above the fireplace. "They are just so majestic. It's amazing how they can spin their heads around two hundred and seventy degrees in either direction."

Ferri monitored Gary, hoping he wouldn't have to babysit the man too much longer. Gary was now alert to his surroundings again and looked at Dr. Bann with narrowed eyes.

Nuriignar joined Dr. Bann in a discussion about the spectacular owls.

Gary huffed and grunted, face twisted in a strange expression. "I'm going for a walk," he said.

Dr. Bann cut short his conversation about owls with Nuriignar and looked at Gary. "Are you sure?" He gestured toward the window at the frigid landscape beyond the cabin walls. "It looks freezing cold outside. Just because I'm a doctor doesn't mean that I am going to save you if something happens."

Gary chuckled, but his face was serious. "Whatever. I'll be back soon. Don't worry, I don't get cold anymore."

Ferri, worried about Gary, followed him out of the cabin door. If Gary noticed, he didn't seem to mind the company. They left the cabin and started walking out onto the frozen lake.

"Where do you think we are?" Ferri asked.

Gary shrugged. "Dr. Bann doesn't know how to use portals that well, so who knew where we are."

'At least we're safe for the moment,' Ferri thought.

Gary walked further out onto the lake ice. The wind had swept away the snow from the surface, and the ice was so clear that he could see straight through to the bottom of the shallow lake. Occasionally, he stumbled upon a frozen fish and looked at it in awe. A living creature, stuck in time. Ferri stood next to Gary and stared at a large fish.

He thought, *'If only I could just freeze time and erase all our problems. That would be great.'*

Taylor got up from a chair in front of the fireplace.

"I'm going to check on Ferri and Gary," he told them. It sounded funny to use the two names in the same sentence.

Nuriignar nodded his bug head, and Dr. Bann waved in acknowledgement. His eyes were closed as he rested in front of the fire.

Just before leaving the cabin, he grabbed a coat off the wall. He wasn't going to be an *idiot* like those other two and suffer the cold outside without proper layers! Beneath the coat, he noticed a Flemett Prison Guard hat hanging on a hook. His eyes widened. Fear returned to his chest—the same fear that he and Ferri had felt after their prison break.

He chose not to inquire further. It wasn't weirder or more puzzling than anything else he'd encountered today.

Outside, he followed the tracks out to the edge of the frozen lake and ventured over to Gary and Ferri, who stood near a glassy, snowless section of the lake. He noticed as he got closer that they were staring intently down into the ice at their feet.

"Find a fish or something?" Taylor asked, feeling the icy wind biting at his exposed face.

Gary and Ferri remained silent.

Taylor stood next to Gary and looked down to check it out. It wasn't a fish.

Frozen in the ice was an owl. Its wings sprawled out as if trapped in endless flight. It was a puzzling display.

"How did that thing get in there?" Taylor asked.

No one replied.

___C___ GARY FELT A warmth wash over him as he stared at the owl in the ice. He thought he saw it move.

Rubbing his eyes, he looked down again and discovered that the owl had disappeared.

He turned to Taylor. "Did you see that? It disappea—"

Taylor stood unmoving, frozen in time.

A voice interrupted his disoriented thoughts. "Don't lose your head, Time Keeper. Your companions will come to rely more and more on your expertise."

Gary searched for the owner of the voice. An owl, like the one he'd seen in the ice, perched atop a snowy branch at the edge of the treeline. Gary moved closer to get a better look.

He realized the voice had come from the owl.

Gary felt suddenly angry. "Time Keeper is what they used to call Jimmy. And he's dead now. What do *you* know?"

The owl blinked and shook snow from its feathers.

"What I know is that Time never forgets its stewards, even when they forget themselves."

Gary noticed that his breath was no longer pluming in the cold air.

"I'm no steward. I'm barely a guy. I have weird Leech and Myst powers. I'm not even the best friend! I've never fixed a single thing I didn't also break first."

The owl tilted its head. "Then you're plenty qualified. Time does not discriminate. It needs hands that have trembled and bled just as readily as the rest."

Gary scoffed. "But Jimmy knew things. He understood this...whatever this Time Keeper role is. Or at least he tried to. He *belonged* to it."

The owl's eyes didn't blink this time. "Jimmy remembered. You're still remembering. That is the only difference."

Gary opened his mouth, then closed it again.

The owl fluttered down to a lower branch, closer now, knocking snow onto the ice below.

"You think Time wants certainty? It prefers those who hesitate. They're less likely to ruin it out of overconfidence. You don't need confidence for this role. You just need to listen to your inner urges."

Gary looked back at Taylor, still frozen mid-blink, caught in a moment that Gary was no longer part of.

Gary sighed, still surprised not to see his breath. "So what do I do?"

The owl looked past him, toward something in the distance. "Keep going. Keep remembering, and when the moment comes, you'll know. Or you won't. Either way, Time will be watching."

The owl lifted off the branch with a silent burst of wings and flew away.

TAYLOR BLINKED, AND THE world resumed.

Gary peered back down into the ice at their feet. The owl had returned to its frozen grave.

He rubbed his temples. He felt overwhelmed, but also felt clearer in his purpose and direction.

___Z___ Gary glanced upward toward Taylor. "This reminds me of something. In Ford's Theater, there was a painting of an owl beside the ticket booth. Jimmy saw an owl in town when we visited the past. In fact, we've seen them often enough that it made me curious. I looked into it."

Taylor and Ferri looked at Gary, hugging themselves against the cold.

"Owls are ancient symbols of wisdom. They bring about change and tell us when things in our lives need attention and adjusting."

He stared at the ice long enough for Taylor to feel impatient as the cold seeped beneath the coat.

"You know, boys," Gary said, resuming, "the Green Skulls are beating us down to stop us from changing the past. And the part of me that is most afraid just wants to cower and listen to them. But I just can't take orders from an evil force. Three of our friends are dead. And those are just the ones we know of. Who knows what happened to everyone else in Jopulous!" He looked up at Taylor and Ferri. "It's time. We have to go back and finish this, once and for all...for all the people we've lost. We have to do exactly what the Skulls don't want us to do."

Taylor and Ferri weren't exactly sure what Gary was talking about, but they nodded. Gary started back toward the cabin, and they followed him, eager to return to the warmth of the hearth.

When they opened the door, a cold gust of wind stirred up the embers of the fire and wafted some ash into the air, startling Dr. Bann and Nuriignar.

Gary addressed the room, sounding brave. "Gents, I know what we need to do. It is—coincidentally—the one thing the Skulls have been telling us *not* to do. We must go back and prevent Lincoln's assassination! We are missing one person, so we'll discuss details when he arrives."

Ferri threw up his arms. "Jimmy is gone, Gary. Remember?"

Gary walked over to a spare bed in the cabin and began clearing it off. "I'm not talking about Jimmy. We are gonna need this extra bed. I'm calling Aair."

"Who?" Ferri asked.

___C___ Aair arrived precisely three seconds after Gary pulsed his brainwaves across the galaxy to summon him.

Aair did not—however—arrive looking like himself. The moment he materialized in front of the group, they let out shrieks and shrunk back, bewildered. Taylor gasped.

Aair looked back and forth at them all, confused.

They all stared at Aair's legs.

Aair looked down, not knowing what to expect. The lower half of his body was absent.

"Oh, *dear!* Not *again*. Please everyone, forgive me!" he said in a tone that Taylor thought was quite nonchalant. "Every now and then when I travel

93

with my belt on too tight, I leave the other half of my body behind. Be right back."

He disappeared once more.

Gary, Ferri, Dr. Bann, Taylor, and Nuriignar looked back and forth at each other. Taylor stared to say what everyone was thinking, but no one had yet said. "What the f—"

Aair rematerialized, cutting off Taylor's exclamation. This time his entire body was intact.

Taylor hadn't met Aair before, but Gary seemed happy to see him.

"Thanks for coming so fast," Gary said.

Aair waved a hand as if to say it was no big deal.

Taylor chimed in. "You look exactly like the first alien girl we met."

Aair brimmed up. "Siiva! Yeah, she's my sister. Where is she anyway?"

Ferri sighed. No other sounds could be heard except the crackling of the fire and a few swallows.

Dr Bann was the first to address the issue. "Aair. Siiva is dead, along with the Ardent, and Jimmy."

A small, sad sound came out of Gary, but no one looked at him. All the focus was on Aair and his reaction to the news.

Slowly, as he processed the event, Aair's face contorted from his usual beaming smile to a dull, empty stare.

"Tell me everything," he said in a demanding voice.

A few minutes later, Dr. Bann finished filling in Aair on the recent events and current situation.

Aair let out a long sigh. "So, let me get this straight. The Green Skulls are going to *kill us all* if we do anything else to alter their ideal timeline. *But,* you guys think it's a good idea to go back into the past to a theater to stop the assassination of some guy that we are all just *assuming* is worth saving? For what?"

The group exchanged glances a few times before Gary finally spoke a reply. "Look, Aair. We all just lost precious friends and family, and I know you don't understand exactly why we are doing this, but we really need your help. We actually *can't* do this without you."

Aair replied, "I *know* you can't do this without me, but I'm still trying to understand it all. Who or what is this benefitting? Why should I help?"

Gary was almost in tears at this point. "I have a good feeling about this, okay? You are just going to have to trust me."

Aair stared at him long and hard as he processed this. "Fine, but only because my sister is dead and I don't want to think about that right now. What is my role in this anyway?"

Gary sat in a chair next to the fire. "Make yourself a chair, Aair," Gary said, shooting a wink at the Flemett boys, who had just learned about Cerebral Solid Creation.

Ferri snickered.

Gary resumed. "So, here's what I think."___**Z**___ "This may be a bit shocking to you guys, if you have any capacity for emotion left after all we've been through. Please take everything I'm about to tell you with a fistful of salt, and I'll try to explain the reasoning behind this escapade within a few minutes."

The group huddled around Gary, their ears awaiting the next batch of informative vibrations to be thrown from his vocal cords.

"Jimmy and I have had many discussions in private over the last few months as to his reasoning behind wanting to stop Lincoln's assassination. He engraved on my mind that I should never tell another soul any of this info. 'You never know who could be a spy,' he would say. I'm telling you anyway, because I need you guys' help. I figure, in order for you to risk your lives, you must know the truth."

Gary looked up at the water-spotted ceiling of the cabin. "Forgive me, Jimmy." Then, returning his gaze to his friends, he spilled the beans.

"President Lincoln was an interesting man. Beloved and detested at the same time—an influential leader. Toward the end of his term, he was stricken with serious heart problems because of a rare inherited disorder known as multiple endocrine neoplasia. Thinking his fate almost sealed, he became fascinated with the idea of time travel. He gathered the best scientists, mechanical engineers, and brainiacs of the era to take part in a massive race against the clock; a race to develop the world's first time-traveling machine before Death paid him a visit."

Nuriignar coughed, drawing eyes, but he waved their attention back to Gary, looking apologetic. Taylor startled at the cough, feeling himself dozing off during Gary's talk. He shook his head, hoping the sleepiness would leave him.

Gary continued. "They were successful, but there was a catch. The machine had yet to be tested on a human subject. Lincoln, well aware that his life's clock would soon strike midnight, told his team of workers to set up the machine in Ford's Theater. He would be the first test subject, and if successful, he'd find a way to prevent himself from developing heart issues in the first place. He did not know how he would do it, but he had a massive team dedicated to answering all the questions. Baby steps."

Gary looked at the faces surrounding him. Everyone appeared to be on the same page.

"Now, how do I know all of this, you might ask? Well, the time-machine was first activated at Ford's Theater, thus opening the first portal into the past for future time-travelers, a.k.a. Jimmy. When Jimmy created his magnificent Tempus Viator, he set the dial back as far as he could and wound up in Ford's Theater, entering the opportunistic space-time rift created by Lincoln's machine."

Taylor felt that the conversation was on the verge of soaring over his head. He barely kept up.

"Jimmy went back repeatedly, waiting for Lincoln to finish watching the show and begin testing his time machine. But it never turned out differently for Ole' Abe. He never made it to the end of the show. Each time, he was killed, and by none other than the *Leader of the Green Skulls*, John Wilkes Booth." He paused to let that sink in.

Jaws dropped around the room. Taylor started to ask a question, but Gary shushed him.

He continued. "Booth was not privy to the fact that if Lincoln had attempted to travel back in time, he would have been unsuccessful. This is because a portal had not been opened prior to that time period. So, Jimmy, after much examination, devised a plan: to stop Lincoln from getting killed, to thwart the agenda of the malicious Green Skulls. Now, my friends, this is our task."

Gary caught his breath and awaited questions from the group. All sound withdrew from the cabin as everyone processed what they had just learned. Taylor didn't feel like asking his questions. No one else seemed confused, so he didn't feel like drawing attention to his own befuddlement.

"Now, I know this is a lot, and I might not have covered every little detail, but you get the gist of it, right? We know now that Lincoln was assassinated by a member of the Green Skulls in order to prevent him from tampering with the past, and we know that Jimmy's plan was to stop Booth from killing Honest Abe. If we can kill the founder of the Green Skulls, maybe we can reverse all the atrocities the Skulls have caused. We just need to think about how we are going to go about all of this."

The bereaved Gary waited patiently for someone to speak up. He looked exhausted and probably needed someone to help him devise a precise plan of action.

Taylor stood up and broke the silence. "I've got it." ___C___ All eyes shifted to Taylor. "Gary, since this was your idea, I say you travel to the theater first to make sure that it is not a trap."

Gary retracted at the statement. "That's *not* a plan. That's a suggestion based on the idea that I might be wrong."

Dr. Bann interjected. "But, Gary, don't you think that could be a possibility?"

Gary raised his voice, his face beginning to change color. "Of *course* it is a possibility, but look at what has happened in the last day alone. *Anything* is a possibility! We can't just refuse to take action because something *might* happen. If we do nothing, then *everyone* who has died will have done so in vain."

Gary took a few deep breaths to calm himself. The color in his face returned to normal.

Nuriignar cleared his throat, as if he had something to say. Everyone looked at him, waiting.

He suddenly seemed caught off-guard. "I just had somethin- in my throat."

Ferri picked up from there. "Look, guys. Gary is right. We've all experienced some heavy loss recently, and we're never going to feel any better unless we do something to bring meaning back to our lives. So, suppose Gary is right. We could change history as we know it! But if we don't do anything, then what?"

Dr. Bann chose this moment to voice a concern. "I think we are overlooking a crucial detail. Suppose we stop the assassination of this Lincoln character. How do we know that the world would be better off if he did not die? What if that is just the way things are supposed to be? What if we actually make things worse?! What if we get killed by the Skulls along with the President? I don't know how I feel about all of this. Haven't you Earth guys ever watched *The Butterfly Effect?*"

"Well, duh, but how do *you* know about that movie?" Taylor asked.

Before Dr. Bann could respond, Nuriignar gasped and pointed at Gary. "-ary! What is happenin- to your arm?!"

Gary looked down. There was a giant symbol on his arm, like a tattoo, that was not there before. It gave off a soft glow in a forest green hue—the same green that colored the fog back in Jopulous.

"It's nothing," Gary said, pulling down his sleeve to cover the strange symbol.

"*Nothing?* Are you serious? Don't you think that is suspicious? It must be the Skulls. Maybe...maybe they are listening? Maybe they know everything!" Taylor said, stammering.

Gary replied, "Taylor. I...don't...care. Maybe I have a death wish, but I will not die standing here talking about what I might have done." He raised his hand. "Who is with me?"

After a few seconds of heavy sighs, a few moans, a couple of F-bombs, and some weird gargling noises from Nuriignar, everyone stepped forward and hesitantly raised their hands.

Gary seemed pleased. "Okay. I think I have it figured out. Here's how we will do it: Aair will relocate us to the theater. We will arrive with enough time to set up before people start filing in to the show. I will get us to a safe spot in the theater where we will not be spotted, but where there is a good view of Lincoln. Then, I will change clothes to blend in, and I will cause an appropriate interference, hopefully stopping or at least distracting Booth. Should I fail, you guys will have to make sure that the assailant does not complete his task. Once the task is complete and Lincoln is confirmed alive, we can decide what to do from there. Questions?"

"Can we sleep on it?" Taylor asked, pointing to the corner of the cabin. "You already got the extra bed ready for Aair."

"If we're gonna do it, we should do it now before the Skulls make the first move!" Gary replied with adamancy.

Taylor couldn't argue with that. He stared with longing at the hearth, wishing he could have at least one night sleeping in front of it.

"Any other questions?" Gary asked.

Heads shook from left to right.

"Aair," Gary said, "it's on you."

THE SHOW

9

AAIR MADE A PORTAL appear, and they began stepping through, one by one.

Gary arrived in the theater first. The play wouldn't be starting for a few hours. The theater was empty.

The others arrived moments later. Taylor noticed a brighter green glow showing through Gary's sleeve. "Gary! Look."

He pulled his sleeve up. The symbol glowed brighter and greener now.

"This is not a cause for concern at the moment. Let's focus on the task at hand. Follow me."

The others did so, but shot nervous glances at each other.

Moments later, they arrived at a dressing room.

Gary opened the door and let everyone inside. "This dressing room belongs to the assailant. I will wait here and subdue him when he enters. He always comes here before the show to get into costume and get his mind straight. You guys can climb this ladder," he said, pointing to the corner. "It should lead to a small viewing area on top of the dressing rooms that is dark and obscured enough to avoid being spotted. We should have a little while before anything happens, so let's go over the plan one more time."

They talked among themselves, making clear all the details of the plan

When three minutes and twenty-six seconds had passed, the dressing room door opened. There was a moment of silent confusion as the group exchanged nervous glances with John Wilkes Booth.

___Z___ "Excuse me, gentlemen, are you not aware that this is my private room?" Booth asked, seeming questionably cool with the present situation.

The group remained silent and began crowding around Nuriignar so that the actor wouldn't notice his alien appearance.

Aair stepped toward Booth and said, "Apologies, good sir. We seem to have a bit of confusion surrounding the current state of events. Allow me to introduce myself and my fellow companions. I am Agent Norman Bridges and this is my team of extraterrestrial exterminators. As you can see, plain as grain, we have apprehended a ferocious creature from Hades itself."

The group, though confused, played along with Aair's little game. They grabbed Nuriignar's arms and began acting as if he was trying to escape. Nuriignar had not caught on yet, so he just stood there, closing his eyes and pretending to be invisible.

Aair cleared his throat, and Nuriignar looked up towards him. A few seconds went by before Nurii processed what was happening.

Suddenly, Nuriignar let out a vicious screech and began flailing around like Jeffrey Dahmer at a morgue.

Aair, actually startled by the performance, began ushering Booth into a corner in order to get him to safety. "Sir, please follow me. We do not need another civilian attack on our record books."

Booth followed Aair into the far corner of the dressing room, just below the ladder leading up to the perch.

During the commotion, nobody noticed that Gary had crept up the ladder and awaited the right moment to strike.

Taylor, Ferri, and Dr. Bann wrestled the belligerent Nuriignar to the ground and tied up all six arms using neckties from Booth's accessory shelf. Aair tried to calm down the actor.

Visibly startled by the incident, John Wilkes Booth sat down on an empty crate and wiped the gathering sweat from his brow. Aair knelt down beside Booth, feigning concern.

"I am *terribly* sorry you had to see that, sir. May I suggest something? I do, in fact, have the supernatural ability to erase a person's recent memories. This could all go away in the blink of an eye."

Booth's breath slowed, and he looked up into Aair's eyes. He got up off the crate and stood face to face with Aair.

Although Aair's outward appearance looked as regular as could be, his trembling eyes threatened to give him away. To a well-versed man like Booth, the eyes and the seemingly harmless joke about mystical powers were enough to trigger the instincts of the Green Skulls leader.

Booth reached into his pocket and wrapped his hand around a switchblade. With his free hand, he shoved Aair to the ground and whipped the knife from his pocket with the other. He charged Aair before he could stand and thrust the blade at his torso. Someone thwarted his attempt, knocking Booth to the ground.

Aair looked up from the floor. Gary stood in front of Booth. A small, red stain grew in diameter on Gary's shirt around the blade of the knife.

Knife in his chest, Gary collapsed to his knees. Aair lunged to cushion the rest of his fall.

Booth sprinted toward the door of the dressing room, but Taylor and Ferri tackled him to the ground.

Dr. Bann rushed over to help Gary. "Alright, lads. We need to get Gary out of here now! Take care of that bastard, Booth, and let's leave this rotten place."

Gary reached up and yanked on Dr. Bann's shirt to bring him in close enough to hear.

"You can't help me, Doc. I have the Mark of the Skulls." He revealed the glowing arm tattoo. "No matter where I go, and no matter what I do, they will always be after me. You guys must finish this here and now. Please!"

Dr. Bann and Aair stood up from Gary's side and walked over towards Booth. Taylor and Ferri had him pinned up against the wall, waiting for further instructions.

Booth cackled like a madman. "You all are pathetic! Killing me won't stop the Skulls. You can never stop the Skulls. We are eternal!"

Suddenly, a high-pitched ringing emitted from a charm around Booth's neck. The ringing was so sharp that it sent everyone in the room into a state of panic. They recoiled into the fetal position and covered their ears, which were beginning to bleed.

Two hours later

AAIR OPENED HIS EYES and peeled his face from the grimy, dressing-room floor. "Guys! Wake up. He is gone."

The rest of the group stirred and rushed over to the door. It was locked.

Ferri noticed the time on a wall-clock. "We have to get out of this room now! The show starts in ten minutes," he said in a frenzy.

He tried to kick the door down.

"Stop!" Gary said with his last bit of energy. "You don't want to bring any attention to yourself. You still have a job to do. I can get the door open."

The group stood around Gary and waited to hear his plan. They heard flesh distorting. Before they realized what was happening, a huge green tentacle shot out of Gary's shoulder and reached up towards the ceiling. The group backed away as Gary used his last ounce of strength to send the tentacle flying towards the door. It broke clean in half, giving them a way out.

"Wow!" Nuriignar said, still in the hiding spot inside of the wine barrel.

Luckily, there was an opening act before Our American Cousin that was quite loud. It had masked the sound of Gary breaking down the dressing-room door.

Aair rushed over to Gary, who wore a huge smile on his face. "Gary, what do we do now?"

Gary coughed up a little blood. He struggled to let out a few more words. "Tell Nuriignar that I'm sorry for scaring him."

Inside the wine barrel, a loud bawling sound echoed.

The rest of the group paid their respects briefly. They still had a task to complete.

Dr. Bann walked over to the barrel that Nuriignar had squeezed himself into. "I need to stay here with this guy until you guys get back. We can't risk him running off and doing something stupid."

A muffled "I'm not stupid" came from inside the barrel in response.

Aair, Taylor, and Ferri looked at each other with determined expressions. No more words needed to be spoken. They changed into outfits that hung on Booth's clothes rack to better blend in. Aair used Cerebral Solid Creation to manifest weapons for the three of them.

Each of them spent a final moment concealing their weapons.

Dr. Bann wished them luck, and the trio left the room to find their places in the theater.

Aair went down to the bottom row, just below the balcony from which Booth always jumped after shooting Lincoln. He would be the last line of defense if Taylor and Ferri failed on the upper balcony.

Ferri and Taylor headed up to the balcony in a calm and collected manner. They took their seats at the very top and focused their gaze on the private box that the president and his guests would soon fill. A few moments of solace passed by before the infamous top-hat of Abraham Lincoln moved into sight at the bottom of the steps. He found his way to his seat.

The show was beginning. The President was in attendance. Now, the only thing left to do was wait for Booth. Taylor and Ferri gave full attention to every single individual who came up the stairs.

Finally, Mr. John Wilkes Booth rounded the corner to ascend the stairs. Taylor and Ferri battled it out in a quick game of rock-paper-scissors to determine who would be the lucky man to battle it out with Mr. Assassinator.

Taylor won.

He stood up and pulled a tiny pink cudgel from his boot.

"Oh, come on," Ferri said in a whisper-shout. "If I had won, Booth would be getting whacked with a Louisville Slugger!"

Taylor turned to look at Ferri. "Where could you possibly be hiding a baseball bat?"

"I was in prison a lot longer than you, pal," he said, joking.

Taylor tiptoed down towards Lincoln's box. He observed Booth take out the security guard, per usual. Then, he saw him duck underneath the curtain, and head into the private box.

Booth placed the smooth barrel against the back of Lincoln's head. "The Green Skulls send their regards!" the Green Skull leader said.

Just before he could squeeze the trigger, a pink cudgel smacked him on the back of the head.

A loud thud sounded, and Booth's limp body crashed to the floor. The theater erupted in panic. Abraham Lincoln stood up and turned to look at Taylor, a look of confusion on his face.

Taylor bowed as if he had just ended a play. "Mr. President, it was an honor."

Everyone in the booth looked perplexed.

Taylor spun around and ran off to find his friends and escape the theater. Behind him, members of the President's party secured Booth to ensure no further threat to Abe if his consciousness returned.

Ferri and Aair met Taylor back in the dressing room as chaos ensued throughout the rest of the theater. With the help of Dr. Bann and Nuriignar, the three began prepping Gary's body for transport back to Jopulous.

Aair opened a portal, and each of the men took turns stepping through. Nuriignar went through first, then Dr. Bann.

As Ferri and Taylor knelt down to grab Gary, they heard footsteps approaching the room.

Aair yelled from halfway inside the portal. "Leave Gary's body. We have no time!"

Despite the pandemonium, Taylor felt the moment stretch out. Thoughts came easily. He felt a sudden urge to stay put. He thought briefly about his and Ferri's imminent return to Earth, even if they were to make it back to the strange world far away. Ferri must have been feeling the same thing. He looked at Taylor and nodded.

With a gigantic sigh, Taylor looked at Aair through the wobbly, mist-like portal and waved his hand.

His voice solemn, he said, "Save yourselves. Rebuild Jopulous. Good-bye."

Aair nodded, saluted, and disappeared. The portal zipped closed just in time.

Five Army officers careened through the broken door of the dressing room and surrounded Taylor and Ferri.

"That's them! They tried to kill the president!"

With no way out, the two rolled their eyes, dropped to their knees, and put their hands on their heads. Before being drug from the room, Taylor looked over to where Gary's body had been lying. It was gone! Only a pool of blood and the switchblade remained.

THE CELL DOOR SLAMMED shut. Taylor sat down on his stone-hard mattress. He heard shouting from the cell across from him. *"C'mon!* I can't catch a break!" the voice said. The voice's owner's back faced Taylor.

Taylor smiled and squeezed his face between the cell-bars. "Ferri? That you, buddy?"

Ferri grabbed the bars of his cell door. "Taylor! I'm having some serious déjà vu! How about you? Once again, we didn't do anything wrong. *Ha!* We don't belong in here, man. Now, we have to escape all over again!"

Taylor gave a sigh of relief. "Glad you are okay. We'll figure it out."

Taylor sat down on the bed and looked at his cleaned and pressed black and white prison uniforms stacked on the bed. Aside from the one he wore now, he had three more. The back of the outfits displayed the words Yemett County Penitentiary.

He stood up and spun around. "How do I look, Kamara?"

Ferri gasped. *"Dude!* There's an owl on the back of your jumpsuit!"

Taylor laughed. "No way! Well, you know what, Ferri? Maybe we *do* belong in here!"

Several Hours Earlier

___C___ GRASCUT RAN HIS hand over the obsidian orb on the table. "Master Phenix," he said, "the other marked one is dead as well."

Marguz smirked. "Very well, mage. Let's hope Jopulous has learned from its mistakes."

"How should we proceed?" Grascut asked.

Before Marguz could respond, a wave of strange energy washed through the hall of the glass castle. Marguz felt...different. Thoughts that had occupied his brain moments earlier had vanished, leaving behind empty voids that quickly filled with questions.

"Grascut," Marguz said in a demanding voice. "What has happened?"

Gruscut stared at the leader of the Skulls. He appeared just as disoriented as Marguz felt.

"Master Phenix," Grascut said, returning to the Eye of the Skulls to find clarity, "it appears that someone has altered the timeline! I cannot be sure who, what, when, why, or how."

Marguz shook his head, feeling suddenly quite annoyed. "So, you know nothing? Is there no way for you to find out what just happened? I feel as though my mind has been wrung out like a wet towel!"

Grascut shot a nervous glance back at Marguz. "Apologies, Master Phenix, but I don't even know where to begin."

Marguz stood from his chair and stormed over to a wall where a knife pinned a picture. The words 'Gary Barnige' hung beneath the picture. Marguz's green brow furrowed as he peered at the photo.

"I will learn who you are and why you are no longer in my memory. Enjoy your life while you have it," he said to the image of Gary Barnige. "Your time is short!"

TO Learn more:

IF YOU'D LIKE TO learn more about the two authors—Cory and Zachary Barber—their creative process, and everything they have to offer (including books, future projects, merch, and more), head over to **wormholebros.com**.

Stay in the loop with everything happening inside the Wormhole by subscribing to the newsletter. Sent out frequently, it offers much more than what's on the website—like access to the **Bonus Content Vault**, where you'll find deep dives into backstories, character interviews, exclusive short stories, and more.

Join the growing crew here: **wormholebros.com/newsletter/**

This page is intentionally blank (well...not anymore), because the printer required an even page count. To make it worth it for the tree that gave it's life for this page, you could draw a picture on it, jot down some notes, or just save the space for autographs at a future author signing event ;)

www.ingramcontent.com/pod-product-compliance
Lightning Source LLC
Chambersburg PA
CBHW071536100726
47908CB00004B/1407